THE DECADENT SPORTSMAN

Medlar Lucan & Durian Gray

THE
DECADENT
SPORTSMAN

Dedalus

**ARTS COUNCIL
ENGLAND**

Published in the UK by Dedalus Limited,
24-26, St Judith's Lane, Sawtry, Cambs, PE28 5XE
email: info@dedalusbooks.com
www.dedalusbooks.com

ISBN 978 1 907650 55 0

Dedalus is distributed in the USA by SCB Distributors,
15608 South New Century Drive, Gardena, CA 90248
email: info@scbdistributors.com   web: www.scbdistributors.com

Dedalus is distributed in Australia by Peribo Pty Ltd.
58, Beaumont Road, Mount Kuring-gai, N.S.W. 2080
email: info@peribo.com.au

First published by Dedalus in 2013
The Decadent Sportsman copyright © *Medlar Lucan & Durian Gray 2013*

The right of Medlar Lucan & Durian Gray to be identified as the authors of this work has been asserted by them in accordance with the Copyright, Designs and Patents Act, 1988.

Printed in Finland by Bookwell
Typeset by Marie Lane

This book is sold subject to the condition that it shall not, by way of trade or otherwise, be lent, resold, hired out or otherwise circulated without the publisher's prior consent in any form of binding or cover other than that in which it is published and without a similar condition including this condition being imposed on the subsequent purchaser.

A C.I.P. listing for this book is available on request.

To Walter and Maria Schnepel

Artists, Patrons, Bearers of the Decadent Light

'the human body, that exquisite engine of delights'

Norman Douglas, *Siren Land*

'...in spite of the tennis the skull alas the stones...'

Samuel Beckett, *Waiting for Godot*

CONTENTS

Foreword	11
Introduction: Mens insana in corpore immundo	13
1 The Fornicast	31
2 The Hydrophile	47
3 The Duellist	77
4 The Rider	107
5 The Gymnast	127
6 The Sculptor of Flesh	149
7 The Fighter	165
8 The New Olympian	197
9 Mind Games	215
Acknowledgements	224
Authors	225

FOREWORD

His Excellency Oscar Luz Morada, Cuban Minister for Sport and Mental Health

In Cuba we take sport seriously. We won an honourable 16th position in the 2012 Olympics, ahead of Spain, South Africa, Mexico, Denmark, Poland, Fiji, Brazil and many other capitalist and imperialist powers. Our athletes are beautiful and strong. Their strength comes from the people. We cultivate the health and athletic skills of our workers, in accordance with the vision of our great Leader Fidel, who was himself a keen gymnast in his youth. In Cuba today all our children spend holidays in sport schools among orange and lemon groves on the Island of Youth. We have swimming pools and baseball stadiums. We have football fields. We have 19,000 boxers and many boxing rings. We send our trainers to work in more than 50 countries.

It is a privilege to have such distinguished personalities as Mr Lucan and Mr Gray sharing their love of sport and art with our people, especially our young people. These two gentlemen have left magnificent careers in England, deserted the fashionable salons of New York, Paris and Milan, and scorned the pages of high-society magazines – why? They do not say. But by their choice to live in Havana they show solidarity with the people of Cuba. They have made the Gimnaseo de Boxeo Guillermo Horta a headquarters of revolutionary artistic thought.

As Minister of Mental Health I must also pay tribute to Mr Lucan and Mr Gray for something else. By their example they have demonstrated that it is possible to live a deranged, eccentric, strangely sexed existence, yet still contribute to our society. The contribution is oblique. It is unusual. But it is real, for they bring hope and glamour to the world's marginals, lunatics, freaks and oddballs – that estimable portion of the human race who feel that conformity is a prison, and who suffer the consequences.

I have read many pages of this beautiful book. I hope to read many more. I recommend it to all those who wish to be free. And to all those who wish to understand the corruption of the capitalist world and its much-vaunted spirit of competition, which leads inevitably to exploitation and slavery. Such criticism from within is more precious than diamonds. As the old Cuban saying goes, there are fifteen ways to make a cigar but only one way to smoke it.

Havana, 27 August 2012

INTRODUCTION: MENS INSANA IN CORPORE IMMUNDO

At first sight, the idea that two such hothouse orchids as Medlar Lucan and I might concern ourselves with Sport seems incongruous in the extreme. The only sort of running either of us has done is that of a bath full of unguents and rose petals; the only time we have vaulted a bar was to get at an exceedingly rare bottle of absinthe we had spotted at Ludovico's in Venice; and the only time we employ 'Higher – Faster – Stronger' is as a mantra in our search for the perfect narcotic.

This is not to say that we are entirely indifferent to sport and sporting events. I have a clear memory of the seminal moment in 2005 when it was announced that London had been chosen as the site for the 2012 Olympic games. Medlar and I had been living in Cuba for several years and we were listening to the news as it came crackling through in Spanish on the radio of our 1961 Pontiac Bonneville while cruising the muddy streets of Baracoa. Both of us were jubilant. Not because we have any particular affection for London. Quite the contrary. The city is nothing more than a collection of undistinguished villages which draws in more and more vulgar spivs every year. No, the reason for our jubilation was the prospect of witnessing a massive expenditure by the capital on an extravagantly pointless event which would have had any heavily bemedalled despot clapping their hands in delight. If ever you are looking for evidence of a nation in decline, the single-minded desire to host a major international sporting event is it. Small wonder that the word 'ludicrous' is derived from the Latin for a game.

At the time of the announcement, of course, conditions were such that the whole project had at least a slim chance of success. The moment was opportune. A buoyant economy. No sign of recession. Imagine, then, our increasing delight as the global economic crisis turned what seemed to be a bold venture into one of supreme foolishness. (It was also at this time, by coincidence, that Medlar was spending more and more time in Greece, the birth canal of the Olympics, watching with fascination as that country sank into a mire of debt). The stage was set for us to sit back and enjoy a performance of hubris and futility by a decayed imperial power which, like Norma Desmond, refuses to believe it is a has-been and embrace its own decline. "Oh, to be a Decadent in such an age when downfalls are everywhere and every inch of common air throbs a tremendous prophecy of greater catastrophes yet to be." This is not exactly what Walt Whitman wrote, but I like to think it is what he meant.

But the question remains: Why this book? What possible link is there between Decadence and Sport?

Before Medlar and I arrived in Havana in early 2000, we would have answered this question with an unequivocal: "There is none". However, our first lodgings in the Cuban capital happened to be a suite of splendidly decrepit rooms on the piano nobile of a crumbling 19th century town house which also housed a fine old Havana boxing club. Up through the floorboards each day drifted the perfume of youthful sweat and leather, the sweet dull sound of padded fist against flesh accompanied by staccato grunts. Each time we passed the massage room on our way out of the building we caught a glimpse of the hardened bodies of young athletes glistening like dark armour stretched out on the tables. Some were injured and receiving treatment. Undoubtedly, there is no more beautiful sight than that of a polychromatic bruise or a bead of blood against dark skin. I was immediately transported back to the time we spent in New Orleans, and in particular to the Fencing School there. It was not long before Medlar and I, irresistibly drawn into the atmosphere of the boxing club, found ourselves acting in an unofficial capacity with regard to its young denizens. We became self-appointed... what? 'Spiritual advisors?' That might be too strong a term, although 'sports psychologists' or 'motivators' would be simply hideous. The correct title does not occur to me at the moment, although we now perform a similar role for a Women's Gymnastics team. More of that anon. Let us return to the subject of bruising.

Pain, the Athlete and the Decadent

One area where the Athlete and the Decadent meet and embrace is on the field of pain. The Athlete confronts pain, courts it, risks it, whether from pushing the body beyond its natural limits, or through violent contact with other bodies. The Decadent likewise embraces pain, seeks it out, whether it is self-inflicted, inflicted by others or on others. Both Athlete and Decadent seek to break through the barrier of pain; the one to gain self-overcoming, the other to find transcendental pleasure. Are not all Athletes masochists at heart?

Ever since my boyhood I have known that writing about and describing the nature of pain is exceptionally difficult, as slippery as the depiction of any ecstatic moment. Some would say that pain destroys language, stops up the voice, makes writing impossible. (Nietzsche could only write by anaesthetising himself with ferocious medicines). Or else it causes the body to revert to the noises and cries which only emerge when language gives out. This is why certain crazed physicians have developed dolorimeters and sonic palpometers to measure pain scientifically. It is noteworthy that the medical profession knows next to nothing about the one thing it deals with daily. This is a bit like the Catholic church admitting that it does not really understand what Sin is. (I can assure you, dear reader, that the Catholic church understands everything there is to understand about Sin). So, in a spirit of investigation, I set myself the task of carrying out some research into the matter of describing pain, which I am sure will make a major contribution to our body of knowledge.

Early on in my searches I came across a very exciting-sounding article on this subject. It was entitled *Camp Sports Injuries: Analysis of Causes, Modes and Frequencies*. I wondered what might count as a 'camp sport', let alone a 'camp sports injury'. Drag queen cage slapping, perhaps? Or feather duster fencing? I imagined the dislocated wrist, the handbag cut, the agony of the broken fingernail or smudged lipstick. In reading the article I found out that it was concerned with injuries sustained by 7 to 15 year-olds in an American summer camp. Here was precisely the sort of academic research for which Medlar and I are particularly well qualified. I lost interest however when I realised that the point of the article was to suggest ways in which such injuries might be prevented.

Next I turned my attention to pain indexes, or indices (depending on whether one protects oneself with Durexes or Durices). Despite the difficulty of giving an accurate account of pain, some have attempted to go even further and to categorise it, to ascribe a value to different levels of pain. One such is the Schmidt index. Designed by entomologist Justin O. Schmidt, it purports to describe and rank the pain experienced from insect bites and stings. Hence:

1.0 Sweat Bee. Light, ephemeral, almost fruity. A tiny spark has singed a single hair on your arm.

1.2 Fire Ant. Sharp: sudden, mildly alarming. Like walking across a shag carpet and reaching for the light switch.

1.8 Bullhorn Acacia Ant. A rare, piercing, elevated sort of pain. Someone has fired a staple into your cheek.

2.0 Bald-faced Hornet. Rich, hearty, slightly crunchy. Similar to getting your hand mashed in a revolving door.

2.0 Yellowjacket. Hot and smoky, almost irreverent. Imagine W. C. Fields extinguishing a cigar on your tongue.

2.2 Honey Bee and European Hornet. Like a match head that flips off and burns on your skin.

3.0 Red Harvester Ant. Bold and unrelenting. Somebody is using a drill to excavate your ingrown toenail.

3.0 Paper Wasp. Caustic and burning. Distinctly bitter aftertaste. Like spilling a beaker of hydrochloric acid on a paper cut.

4.0 Tarantula Hawk. Blinding, fierce, shockingly electric. A running hair drier has been dropped into your bubble bath.

4.0+ Bullet Ant. Pure intense brilliant pain. Like fire-walking over flaming charcoal with a 3-inch rusty nail in your heel.

This index is of course absurd, a mixture of hyperbole and the surreal, accompanied by a numerical value which relates to nothing at all. It fails to convey even a vague sense of the nature of pain. This is because it is obviously not rooted in personal experience. How can Herr Schmidt possibly know what it feels like to fire-walk with a three inch rusty nail in his heel? Besides, the whole point about fire-walking is that the walker feels no pain. No, this won't do.

A more engaging read is the McGill index which goes to the opposite extreme, attempting to furnish a broad, common vocabulary for levels of pain. Sufferers are presented with a list of adjectives to choose from:

Flickering, Pulsing, Quivering, Throbbing, Beating, Pounding
Jumping, Flashing, Shooting
Pricking, Boring, Drilling, Stabbing
Sharp, Cutting, Lacerating
Pinching, Pressing, Gnawing, Cramping, Crushing
Tugging, Pulling, Wrenching
Hot, Burning, Scalding, Searing
Tingling, Itchy, Smarting, Stinging
Dull, Sore, Hurting, Aching, Heavy
Tender, Taut (tight), Rasping, Splitting
Tiring, Exhausting
Sickening, Suffocating
Fearful, Frightful, Terrifying
Punishing, Gruelling, Cruel, Vicious, Killing
Wretched, Blinding
Annoying, Troublesome, Miserable, Intense, Unbearable
Spreading, Radiating, Penetrating, Piercing
Tight, Numb, Squeezing, Drawing, Tearing
Cool, Cold, Freezing
Nagging, Nauseating, Agonising, Dreadful, Torturing

Reading this index reminds me of a weekend house party which Medlar and I attended recently in Montevideo. It is more of menu than a description. One could imagine arriving at one of Berlin's more recondite establishments and ordering 'some no. 4 followed by no. 10 and a side order of no. 20.' But again, this index is too inconsistent. How can pain be simultaneously 'annoying' and 'unbearable'? The problem with these indexes is that they are all terribly negative. They fail to register, or even acknowledge, the extent of pleasure which can be derived from pain.

In response to the inadequacy of existing indexes, my own efforts in this area have resulted in the Lucan and Gray Colour-Coded Index of Decadent Pain, based largely on E. M. Cioran's idea that the limit of every pain is an even greater pain. The index reads thus:

Blue – this is the level of pain which evokes the involuntary gasp, the uncontrolled whimper, a point at which the body speaks directly without the will of the speaker. Medlar is very keen on the distinction between pain which causes an inhalation, as if the body wants to take in the intensity to control it, and pain which causes an exhalation, as if the body wants to expel the sensation. For the Decadent of course the former is by far the preferable course of action. Anyone who has felt the spiteful bite of the cane will recognise this.

Green – tears and sweetness. Often this level of pain is accompanied by other physical sensations such as the scent of rotting lilies or a feeling of sanctity. This pain can be administered by somebody close to you, or else a stranger. It results in feelings of deep-seated gratitude towards the perpetrator. The narrator of *Venus in Furs* writes: "The blows fell rapidly and powerfully on my back and arms. Each one cut into my flesh and burned there, but the pains enraptured me. They came from her whom I adored, and for whom I was ready at any hour to lay down my life".

Black – dark pain. Depression and fear and anxiety. It becomes a companion and tormentor, one which never leaves your side. You may attempt to befriend it. You may even take it as a lover, in the hope that this will transform it in some way. The horror of this pain is that it has no source and no cause.

Red – the scream. This is that pain which one feels of such intensity that it leaves one teetering on the edge of the abyss, quite uncertain as to whether or not one will plunge headlong into unconsciousness. It is that liminal state across which the spirit wanders back and forth, like a brain-damaged boxer.

Purple – the moment of sublime beauty. The moment when pain becomes so intense that it surpasses all understanding and perception. It is no longer something that happens to the body; it is the body. This is the point where pain is both closest and furthest away. In other words it is where pain threatens to become transcendent, or even sublime. To misquote Antoine Artaud:

The purple horror
Of exceeding oneself
In that extreme pain
Which will no longer be pain in the end.
That is what I never stopped thinking.

White – this is the rarest and most exquisite of the stages. The moment should be looked out for and yet any anticipation of white pain will change its nature. The body has to be taken unawares. Often it lasts little more than a second or two and it precedes a loss of consciousness. At first there appears to be no pain at all. There is a moment of great calm, like the eye of a storm, before an explosion of hurt where the body, the mind, and the soul disappear. The degree of pain experienced is such that it fills the entire universe.

The more perceptive reader will have noticed that as an ensemble these colours constitute the spectrum of a bruise on the skin of a red-haired woman. In my experience red-heads are not only peculiarly susceptible to livid bruising, which the more intriguing among them rejoice in, but also their particular bluish-white complexion acts as a perfect setting for the myriad colours of subcutaneous bleeding.

But let us consider further this connection between Sport and Masochism. With regard to the latter, some of the most spectacular and ruthless masochists in history have been Christian saints and mystics. In certain respects they are quintessentially Decadent characters. St Margaret Mary Alacoque remarked that 'None of my sufferings has been equal to that of not suffering enough'. One of Eckhart's pupils, Blessed Henry Suso, designed and wore a special undergarment lined with 150 sharpened nails that constantly pierced his skin; a sort of super-cilice. He also wore gloves lined with sharp tacks intended to prevent him from picking off the lice and other insects that fed on his body. And when it comes to a description of Saintliness, we can do no better than to return to E. M. Cioran. According to this latter-day Nietzsche, Saintliness cannot exist without the voluptuousness of pain and a perverse refinement of suffering. Furthermore, he sees sanctity as a special kind of madness; '...while the madness of mortals exhausts itself in useless and fantastic actions, holy madness is a conscious effort towards winning everything'.

Our contention is that the Athlete, whose sport is often referred to as a 'vocation', is consumed by this form of holy madness. According to Cioran, next to the mystic, the Saint is the most active of men. The Saint is also the source of all tears. He writes: 'As I searched for the origin of tears, I thought of the Saints... To be sure, tears are their trace'. And how closely associated are tears with sport! How often do we see our Athletes dissolve into tears before our very eyes after their moment of extreme exertion! (Medlar once had a mistress who responded in the same way). What was formerly considered a reprehensible and self-aggrandising display is now compulsory in the sporting world. Tears must accompany triumph and failure alike. Superficially they are said to bear witness to an outpouring of emotion experienced after testing the body to the limit. However, my sense is that the tears of the Athlete are related to a reconnection with the decadence of Medieval religiosity and a deep-seated sense of the Loss of Paradise. I find this thesis compelling and cogent, although there are some senior theologians who think it over-stretched.

Mention of Medlar's erstwhile mistress leads me seamlessly to another gilded couch upon which the Decadent lies down with the Sportsman: breathlessness. Any of us who have engaged in auto-erotic asphyxiation will recognise the sensual attraction of that state where the Athlete, at the end of a contest, is gasping for breath, desperate to revive an oxygen-starved system. This is very close to the ideal conditions for an orgasm of great intensity. The condition of extreme breathlessness links the Athlete to de Sade, who in *Justine* describes a scene where Thérèse's master, Roland, foresees pellucidly his destiny – dancing at the end of the hangman's rope. In order to face this fate with equanimity, he needs to know whether the accounts of erotic stimulation which accompany hanging are true or not. And he tells Thérèse that she has to help him in this. She relates the outcome thus:

We take our stations; Roland is stimulated by a few of the usual caresses; he climbs upon the stool, I put the halter round his neck; he tells me he wants me to curse him during the process, I am to reproach him with all his life's horrors, I do so; his dart soon rises to menace Heaven, he himself gives me the sign to remove the stool, I obey; would you believe it, Madame? nothing more true than what Roland had conjectured: nothing but symptoms of pleasure ornament his countenance and at practically the same instant rapid jets of semen spring nigh to the vault. When 'tis all shot out without any assistance whatsoever from me, I rush to cut him down, he falls, unconscious, but thanks to my ministrations he quickly recovers his senses.

"Oh Thérèse!" he exclaims upon opening his eyes, "oh, those sensations are not to be described; they transcend all one can possibly say: let them now do what they wish with me, I stand unflinching before Themis' sword!"

In our relentless pursuit of scientific knowledge, Medlar and I have approached the Universidad de la Revolución with a proposal to carry out controlled experiments on some undergraduate volunteers comparing the breathlessness of Athletes at the end of a sprint with that of male or female subjects at the moment of orgasm. Our findings will be published in a suitable journal as soon as we have them.

Voyeurism

Now, before any sports enthusiast jogs up to us and tosses the accusation that our research is nothing but voyeurism, which given Medlar's pedigree is not an unreasonable accusation, I would point out that modern sport and voyeurism are kissing cousins. One might say they are engaged in an act of mutual masturbation. For every participant in a sport there are countless numbers for whom sitting back and watching is about as much as they are capable of. Nowadays, the sum total of exercise for many consists in lifting and pulling the metal ring in a can of beer-flavoured urine before collapsing back onto the couch. Barely able to raise their obese frame from the sofa where they sprawl, they spend their money and time on watching magnificently honed bodies exerting themselves to the point of collapse. Whether the setting is that of a stadium or a pornographic film studio, it matters little. To paraphrase Villiers de l'Isle-Adam: 'Living? We leave our 42 inch plasma television to do that for us.' Scopophilia is the single greatest participatory sport, and this is all part of the continuing 'Caligulisation' of the common man, as Medlar has expressed it, and in which we are proud to be playing a small part.

Victor Ludorum/Defectio Ludorum

Given the erotic charge of the sight of any breathless Athlete, the relentless focus of interest on the victor in any sporting event makes no sense from the Decadent's point of view. And the banalities uttered by winners in the wake of their victory are by far the least interesting aspect of any sporting spectacle. Far more entrancing are the utterances of those who have collapsed from severe oxygen debt, who have given every last ounce of effort after years of training and blind self-sacrifice, and have come fifth. Failures intrigue us. The Decadent can best relate to those who look back on a life wasted in pursuit of a goal which always evaded them and who can only cope with this through a process of self-delusion. "It's the taking part that is important. It's been a wonderful experience I'll never forget..." they mumble with melancholic lack of conviction. This is their motto:

Defectio mihi robur dat. Dolor est ratio mea.

'Failure is my strength, pain is my motivation', and not in a positive way. From a Decadent's point of view, this all makes little sense. Rather than this desperate attempt to give meaning to the wasted existence of the runner-up, why not glory in the abject humiliation of defeat? We turn again to Sacher-Masoch for enlightenment...

"Now watch me break him in," said the Greek. He showed his teeth, and his face acquired the blood-thirsty expression, which startled me the first time I saw him.

And he began to apply the lash – so mercilessly, with such frightful force that I quivered under each blow, and began to tremble all over with pain. Tears rolled down over my cheeks. In the meantime Wanda lay on the ottoman in her fur-jacket, supporting herself on her arm; she looked on with cruel curiosity, and was convulsed with laughter.

The sensation of being whipped by a successful rival before the eyes of an adored woman cannot be described. I almost went mad with shame and despair.

What was most humiliating was that at first I felt a certain wild, supersensual stimulation under Apollo's whip and the cruel laughter of my Venus, no matter how horrible my position was. But Apollo whipped on and on, blow after blow, until I forgot all about poetry, and finally gritted my teeth in impotent rage, and cursed my wild dreams, woman, and love.

And what of the victors? What is their legacy, other than that brief moment of triumph? The only function of the triumph is to highlight the decline, the darkness, the years of embittered self-loathing that so often follow in the wake of that moment in the sun. Triumph simply serves to increase the distance that the victor has to fall in the aftermath of a lofty achievement. Witness the case of Dave Duerson, a legendary American football player with an eleven year career. He was twice in a winning Superbowl team. Charismatic, tall, beautiful, articulate and charming. After he left the sport he became a successful businessman. Then, within a few years he had gone bankrupt, been divorced and was fighting his ex-wife in court. He suffered from lapses in memory, mood swings, piercing headaches on the left side of his head, had difficulty spelling simple words, and his eyesight was blurred. On 17 February 2011, aged fifty, Duerson shot himself through the heart; deliberately, according to the suicide note he left, so as to leave his brain undamaged. This he donated to medical research. This organ, like the brain of many retired footballers and Decadents, showed signs of dramatic neuro-degeneration. Failure is so much more subtle and complex than victory. Let the Athlete join his brother the Decadent in embracing it with breathless ecstasy.

W

Haunting the pages of this book will be another: the extraordinary vision promulgated by Georges Perec in *W, or the Memory of Childhood*. Crossword compiler, archivist, flâneur long before and after it was fashionable, chronicler of the infra-ordinary and formalist experimenter, Perec is about as far removed from the idea of the Decadent writer as possible. However, for his infernal vision of the ultimate sports-centred society, he is admitted to the Pantheon.

The W of the title refers to an island...

Tradition has it that the founding, and indeed the very name, of the island can be traced back to somebody by the name of Wilson. Although this origin is agreed on by all, there are a number of variations... A fourth variation, [...] makes Wilson a champion (some say a trainer) gripped by the idea of the Olympics; but as he had been disheartened by the difficulties which Pierre de Coubertin had had to face at that time, and convinced that the Olympic ideal could be derailed, corrupted and distorted by sordid trade-offs and compromises unacceptable to the very people who claimed to serve it, Wilson decided to do all that was humanly possible to found a new Olympia far removed from nationalistic squabbles and ideological machinations.

...But it doesn't make much difference whether W was founded by outcasts or sportsmen. What is true, what is undeniable, what is immediately striking, is that today W is a land where Sport is king, a nation of Athletes where Sport and Life are united in a single magnificent

endeavour. The proud motto:

FORTIUS ALTIUS CITIUS

carved on the monumental arches at the gates of every village, the splendid stadiums with their meticulously maintained cinder tracks, the gigantic notice board where the results of sporting contests are published hour by hour, the celebrations held daily for the winners, the men's dress: grey tracksuits with a large W emblazoned on the back, these are the sights which greet the newly arrived visitor. From them, he will understand with wonderment and enthusiasm... that life, here, is lived for the greater glory of the Body. And it will later be seen how the athletic vocation shapes the life of the State, how Sport rules W, how it has determined every aspect of social relations and individual ambitions.

You, dear reader, will catch glimpses of Perec's vision of the true hell of such a society, one which values Sport as its highest ideal, where competition pervades all aspects of everyday life, where Victory is the only moment of value and where the term 'loser' is just about the worst insult you can hurl at anybody.

1

THE FORNICAST

Position Paper sent to the International Olympic Committee on the Inclusion of Sexual Athletics (Fornicastics) as Recognised Sports in Future Olympic Games

Authors
Medlar Lucan and Durian Gray (unofficial advisors to the Cuban Olympic Women's Gymnastic Team).

Summary
The aim of this paper is to promote the introduction of all forms of competitive copulation into the portfolio of sports on display at the Olympic Games. It is conceived under the auspices of the Féderation Internationale de Copulation Athlétique (FICA).

Argument
Our contention is that sex fulfils many if not all of the present criteria for inclusion as laid out in the Olympic charter. It is also one of the world's most popular sporting activities.

Organisation
One of the major demands of the International Olympic Committee is that there is a governing body for each sport that oversees all aspects of its organisation and management. We

can assure the IOC that we, Medlar Lucan and Durian Gray, have recently formed such a Governing Body, the Féderation Internationale de Copulation Athlétique (FICA), registered at the Municipality of Havana, Cuba, in January 2012. Our legal team is at present working on the details of the constitution. These are some of the major decisions made by FICA:

i Professionalism
It has been voted upon and decided by the Committee, true to the spirit of the Baron de Coubertin's initial vision for the Games, that Fornicastics will be an all-amateur affair. Any participant who can be shown to have taken payment for their sport will render themselves inadmissible for the games and place themselves outside the jurisdiction of the FICA. This category includes striptease and burlesque artistes, pornographic film actors, gigolos, pimps, *madames*, pole-dancers, catamites, professional dominatrices, hustlers, prostitutes and sex-workers in general. This will not apply to writers, photographers or artists' models, however. We are keen to maintain the amateur ethos in all its purity and are compiling a definitive list of those who may and who may not participate in events, while admitting that there will be grey areas; for example, male and female escorts.

ii Doping and performance-enhancing substances
FICA will work closely with WADA (World Anti-doping Agency) to ensure that all competitors in the Fornicastics events are 'clean'. FICA will ensure that no aphrodisiacs will feature in the events, whether these take the form of amyl nitrate, viagra, ginger, chillies, nettles, Mama Juana, extract of rhino horn, donkey testicles, deer antlers, tiger's penis, tongkat ali, ashwagandha, rhodiola, catuaba, yohimbe, maca, eleuthero,

saw palmetto, borojo, ginseng, arginine, Mucuna pruriens, Tribulus terrestris, Epimedium grandiflorum, Spanish fly, or other performance-enhancing drugs or preparations, derived from whatever sources, whether animal, vegetable, mineral or chemically synthesised. We have taken on Dr Rebecca Stevenson of the Institute of Sports Meteorology to elaborate a series of tests in partnership with us to assess the efficacy of these preparations, which will be used in the pursuit of those who seek to take unfair advantage.

iii Levels of Inclusivity and Participation
This point hardly needs arguing. The participants can be counted in their billions. However, some might argue that their participation is too informal (or conversely too formal) to be counted. FICA would accept this. A suitable analogy might be the difference between bike riding and cycling. Whereas riding a bike is a pastime and hobby, cycling is what is properly deemed to be a sport. Similar distinctions can be drawn up in sexual activity, which can be practised in a haphazard, opportunistic manner, or as a serious competitive sport, and indeed at various levels of engagement in between. However, once we have formalised the competitive element of Fornicastics and achieved Olympic status, we are confident that theoretical questions of definition and categorisation will melt away in the blaze of public enthusiasm.

An important element of our proposal is that the sport will question the traditional barriers between male and female competitors, in many cases overturning them altogether. As we envisage it, all sexes will be able to compete on equal terms-together, separately and in team activities. This also holds true of gay, lesbian, trans-sexual, poly-sexual and disabled competitors. No more need for a separate Paralympian event.

iv Venues

The question of venues remains open and many-sided. A range of venues is conceivable, from the intimate (bedchamber, wagon-lit, pantry, aeroplane toilet, understairs cupboard) to the public (cinema, concert hall, fire-station, etc), to the open air (woodland, cave, sea-shore, desert, mountain...). Custom-built spaces may at some future date be required; words for such structures exists in French – *baisodrome, tringlodrome* – and where the word exists there is every likelihood that the reality will follow. No doubt as the sport develops, there will be a corresponding need for the development of new scenarios and contexts as competitors attempt more and more imaginative and demanding routines.

v Nomenclature

The events are grouped by FICA under ten general headings:

Individual fornicastics (formerly termed masturbastics)
Singles or Foutrage (Men's, Women's, Mixed)
Doubles or Partouse (Men's, Women's, Mixed)
Team or Gruppenschaft (Men's, Women's, Mixed)

Under each heading, the single events are as follows:

Classical, Rustic, Freestyle, Corinthian, Weird, Bestial, Taboo, Ecclesiastical, Historical, Futuristic.

This gives a working total of one hundred events.

vi. Laws and Scoring system

We would like to assure the committee from the outset that

Fornicastics, far from being a random and disorderly activity, can be, and indeed already has been, exquisitely codified. We set out below a rational organisation of the activities based on the thinking of the universally acknowledged forefather of sexual athletics, Donatien Alphonse François, Comte de Sade.

The Laws
Taking the activities of the inmates of the Château de Silling as a model, we have organised the sport according to a blueprint laid down by de Sade in *120 Days of Sodom*. The smallest unit of erotic activity is the *posture*; this comprises just one bodily action and its point of application. Postures are not restricted to sexual acts on the part of the Athlete, but can include such things as his or her examination of the partner/victim, interrogation, the uttering of obscenities or blasphemy etc. It is possible to enumerate each posture and to apply a value or score to them. As the posture is an action that is often repeated, its score can be assessed. For example, in de Sade, after an orgy involving Juliette, Clairwil, and the Carmelites one Easter, Juliette calculates that she has been had 128 times one way, 128 times another way, thus 256 times in all. A scoring value can easily be ascribed to each of these postures.

De Sade goes on to explain that units of higher value can be created by combining a number of postures into an *operation*. The operation calls, at least most frequently, for several athletes, and when it is conceived as a sequence, developing in time through a succession of postures, it is called an *episode*. However, when the postures are performed simultaneously ie when it is conceived as a tableau, it is called a *figure*. What limits (and constitutes) the episode are the constraints of time (the episode is contained between two ejaculations); what limits the figure are the constraints of space (all erotic sites must be simultaneously occupied). Finally, operations, extending and succeeding each other, form the largest possible unit of this erotic syntax, the *scene* or *séance*.

Added to these units are two principal laws of action. The first is a rule of exhaustiveness: in an "operation," the greatest number of postures must be simultaneously achieved; this implies on the one hand that every athlete present be occupied at the same time, and on the other hand, that in each subject every part of the body should be 'erotically saturated'. In *120 Days of Sodom,* the finest example of this is the scene which involves Juliette, cardinals Bracciani and Chigi, Olympe Borghese, the confederates, a monkey, a turkey, a dwarf, a child, and a dog.

The second rule of action is the rule of reciprocity. In the *scene*, all functions can be interchanged. Every athlete must be in turn agent and patient, whipper and whipped, coprophagist and coprophagee, sodomist and sodomised, active and passive, etc. This is the basis of a more elaborated system of formal rules governing the performance and scoring of Fornastics which we would be pleased to present to the committee at their convenience.

Scoring will be the main area of contention in Fornicastics. The scoring systems will draw largely upon those used in gymnastics, diving, dressage and figure skating, with marks awarded by two panels of judges, the 'D' panel for the difficulty, requirements and connections of a routine, and the 'E' panel for its execution and artistry. Various stages of the routine are judged and scores aggregated. To take an example, the Rustic Routine is defined as consisting of the following twelve stages: the Starting Position, the Approach, the Arousal, the Mount, the Entry, the Frottage, the Pistonage, the Temporary

Withdrawal, the Reversal, the Re-Entry (or Alternative Entry), the Dismount, and the Cigarette.

Numerical values, often a matter of controversy, are based on an unimpeachably objective source: the bill of tariffs of a Peking gentlemen's brothel. These are listed in the opening chapter of *Décadence Mandchoue* by the celebrated sinologist, spy and forger, Sir Edmund Backhouse. The setting is the 'Hall of Chaste Joys', the year 1899. The managing director, Tsai Mu, explains the system:

> *Simple or unipartite copulation with the pathic [passive partner] costs Taels 30; reciprocal copulation costs Taels 45;* P'in Hsiao *(flute savouring, in allusion to the shape of a Chinese flute which resembles the male organ) or* fellatio *is Taels 10 extra if limited to the pathic; Taels 15 if practised by the latter on the client;* irrumatio *or* coitio per buccam *is Taels 30 inclusive of* Feuilles de Rose, *or what we call "Cinnamon Leaves",* Kuei Yeh, *if applied by the client to the pathic's anal, pubic and perineal region but if the client requires this labial business on his verge, posterior, etcetera, he must disburse Taels 45. If the client's passions are dull and he needs aphrodisiac stimulation,* Vyenki *[rods for whipping] are available. To be chastised by the selected pathic, charges vary according to the severity of the whipping. Usually, added Mr Tsai with a meaning grin, twelve strokes makes the client call "Halt": he must pay a minimum of Taels 12 for a normal flagellation and Tael 1 for the* Vyenki, *which, of course, breaks under use. If he is unsated after twelve strokes, he must pay Tael 1 per* Hieb *[blow]. But if the client desires to retaliate on the buttocks of the pathic, he must pay an extra Taels 45*

as a personal compensation for the catamite's broken skin and a nominal fee to the establishment of Taels 5 plus Tael 1 for each Vyenki *as aforesaid. The catamite's pudenda (Ch'iao Tzu or penis, "cunning tool") testicles (Tan Tzu), anal region, fundament and perineum are all delicately perfumed and, as goes without saying, kept most scrupulously clean: the pubic and anal hair is clean shaven like the face. Naturally, if the client desires intimate labial contact on his person, he will wish to perform appropriate ablution on his secret parts. An exquisite scent from Java (or Borneo) is available for Taels 5 a bottle; so that the practical and aesthetic side of what might appear gross and physical (even filthy) be not neglected. However, you shall have everything for a fixed tariff of taels 50, plus a fee for the "pleasuring" to him whom you deem worthy of your regard.*

FICA accepts that there is a great deal of detailed work still to be done on this submission. However, it hopes that this initial paper will provide the blueprint for further fruitful negotiations with the IOC and we may look forward to a happy outcome to this proposal.

Medlar Lucan
Durian Gray
Havana, August 2012

Historical Note

The links between sport and sex go back centuries, although the relationship between the two has always been confused and sometimes contradictory. Over time and in different cultures the argument has been whittled down to two conflicting points of view. The first states that sport is simply a variant on sex. One only has to look at the way American football is presented – a spectacle of openly homo-erotic violence punctuated by lascivious displays from barely pubescent girls in flimsy clothing – to realise that this is the case. The second, particularly fashionable during the ascendency of the Prude, holds up sport as a healthy and highly acceptable alternative to sex, one that dissipates the sexual drive.

If we take the latter argument first, we may note that long before Freud (or more precisely, Nietzsche) came up with the idea of 'sublimation', everybody from the Greeks to English public school masters to adherents of the Hindu discipline of Brahmacharya knew that participation in sport, alongside cold showers and rubbing the lower part of the abdomen or belly with a coarse Turkish towel, is one of the most effective ways of stemming nocturnal emissions. It is a well-attested fact that there is often something of an antagonism between sexual activity and sport. Sportsmen, in particular, are commonly advised to refrain from sexual activity before competition. There is a good deal of evidence that the two are not mutually beneficial. However, in his constant and unquenchable quest for knowledge, Prof. Medlar Lucan has recently undertaken some interesting experiments with the aim of ascertaining the truth of this proposition. In conjunction with a researcher from the Massachusetts Institute of Sexology, Prof. Lucan subjected himself during a period of three weeks to a programme of furious sexual congress and relentless onanism. At the end of this time, his vital signs – resting heart rate, blood pressure, colour of urine, etc. – were monitored and recorded. He then engaged in a bout of Greco-Roman wrestling with Alex Morvanescu, a 14-stone Romanian ex-champion. He was soundly beaten by his opponent in a matter of minutes. *Prima facie,* this would seem to support the case for the adverse effects of sexual activity on sporting performance. However, Prof. Lucan then undertook an extended period of sexual abstinence which was accompanied by birchings, cold baths, a daily bromide cocktail and the wearing of a spiked cock ring, all designed to eliminate even the thought of sexual activity. At the end of this period, Prof. Lucan again stepped into the Greco-Roman arena with Alex the Romanian. He was, much to his delight, soundly beaten again. Prof. Lucan is of the opinion that these preliminary findings point to the fact that sexual abstinence has no significant effect on sporting performance. However, he concedes that there is more research to be done. To this end, Lucan and Gray are hoping to find a benefactor who would underwrite the establishment of an Institute of Sport Sex Research in partnership with what they describe as one of most prestigious universities in South America.

On the other side of the argument, the historical record compels us to observe that sporting and sexual performance often go hand in hand. Expertise in one leads to proficiency in the other. Jackie Stewart, the Scottish racing driver who swept all before him in the 1970s, made some revealing remarks on this subject. Explaining his technique of cornering at high speed, he begins by comparing a Formula 1 car to a racehorse:

A Formula 1 car is really an animal; a machine, yes, of course, but beyond that an animal because it responds

> *to different kinds of treatment. A highly bred racehorse, a thoroughbred in its sensitivity and nervousness. To get the best out of it you must coax it, treat it gently and sympathetically. In a corner it's right on its tiptoes, finely balanced, on the very edge of adhesion, just fingertips on the road, and if you dominate it or try to push it around, it will go straight on or slide off or do any number of things that leave you without control. So you coax it – gently, very gently – to get it to do what you want.*

Now the language becomes more erotic. At first this is implicit:

> *You point it and coax it into the apex, and even after you've pointed it and it's all set up, committed to the corner which might be fifty or a hundred feet away, you must be tender with it, holding it in nicely, because it's got an angle on it, an angle of roll, and it's building to its climax of hitting that apex. You've set a rhythm and now you must keep it. And as it hits the apex you take it out nicely; you don't say, "You've got your apex, now I'll put my boot in it and drive however I want." No, your exit speed is very important, so you've got to maintain that balance or rhythm which you've been building all along. You've got to follow through, let the car fulfil itself.*

Then the sexual parallel is made explicit:

> *Cornering is like bringing a woman to a climax. The two of you, both you and the car, must work together. You start to enter the area of excitement of that corner, you set up a pace which is right for the car, and after*

you've told it that it's coming along with you, you guide it through at a rhythm which has by now become natural. Only after you've cleared that corner can you both take pleasure in knowing that it's gone well. If you do otherwise, alter the car's line, sometimes by no more than three or four inches, scrape a curbing, give it too much throttle or fail to feed it in gently, you'll spoil it. You'll ruin it. Through your own impatience you'd have taken away all the pleasure.

Long before the invention of the internal combustion engine there were many for whom sex was an indispensable part of a daily work-out. It consumed their lives in the same way that sport consumes the lives of top athletes, and with similarly energising effects.

Catherine the Great, Empress of Russia, is a case in point. She grew tired of her dreary and oppressive husband, the Emperor Peter III, and, having deposed him from the throne, took on a succession of lovers, including Stanislaw August Poniatowski, Grigory Orlov and Grigory Potemkin. She liked military men, of proven courage, with quick, practical minds. Her correspondence reveals the strong romantic element in her affairs; although a keen and vigorous fornicator, she was not the lust-crazed nymphomaniac of vulgar repute.

Nor was that other legend of the eighteenth century bedchamber, Giacomo Casanova. An aristocratic rake, traveller, gambler and spy, he was a contemporary of Catherine (they met in Riga and St Petersburg, but their intercourse was purely social). His memoirs, compiled at the Castle of Dux in Bohemia in his old age, are a rich manual of sexual athletics, filled with wise advice and illuminating anecdotes. The famous competition scene in Federico Fellini's film *Casanova* is a felicitous invention by the scriptwriter, Bernardino Zapponi, but it encapsulates the great athlete's spirit perfectly. At a party in Rome, a coachman claims to have had sex seven times in one day.

"He's lying," says Casanova. "Brute force alone is incapable of such amatory prowess... Only a body sustained by wit, intelligence and culture can reach the peaks. Let me tell you why. It requires considerable moral maturity, to say nothing of inspiration, knowledge of the movements of fluids, of stellar and planetary influences; it requires, above all, imagination."

Lord Talou, the host, is intrigued. "Why not have a challenge – brute force versus intelligence, the 'noble savage' exalted by that bore Rousseau against a man of rank and culture?"

Casanova is unwilling to take part in such a crude display, but a Neapolitan duchess begs him to change his mind: it will be, she says, a contest between vulgarity and poetry.

Casanova accepts, and orders some sustenance: a basket of fresh eggs, a bottle of Spanish wine, ginger, cinnamon, cloves. The consorts are chosen, the contestants undress, and the battle begins... The coachman, despite his large, rustic *membrum virile* and an eager partner, manages only three climaxes before collapsing. Casanova, the long-distance man, is just getting into his stride.

One could enumerate many more such figures: Frank Harris, the Marquis de Sade, Bertrand Russell, Frieda Lawrence, Kenneth Clark, John F. Kennedy, Malcolm Campbell, Gabriele D'Annunzio, Mae West, Lillian Hellman... but the point is surely made. By bringing sexual athletics into the Olympic arena, we may also do a great service to humanity, worthy of Pierre de Coubertin – to settle, once and for all, the opposition that exists between those who believe that sex is the antagonist of sporting achievement, and those who see it as its apogee, its triumph, its vital and perfecting partner.

2

THE HYDROPHILE

17th May 1849. A grassy river bank near London. In the failing evening light, a slight, pale, naked boy scrambles out of the water, his body ghostlike in the darkening air. He stands for a moment, dripping and shivering. He glances nervously about, alert as a bird. The meadows around him are deserted. The sky is a vermilion canopy streaked with purple and livid blue. He feels alone, free, invulnerable. On an impulse he begins to run along the bank. The air is cold on his wet body. Droplets of water fly off him. His bare feet crush the cool turf.

He reaches an oak tree, a vast fungus of shadow. He circles it, mothlike, skipping in and out of its penumbra, to a music that sounds in his mind; shrieking flutes, drums that clatter and thunder, trumpets that blaze like the Aegean sun. He flings his arms to the sky, throws back his head, skips and spins on his toes, a whirling propeller, a floating sycamore seed, spinning, spinning, the twilight fields, riverbank and trees a rotating vision, blurred with speed, until vertigo claims him, he spirals to the ground, panting. He stretches full length, at the edge of the shadow, beneath the outermost branches. His head is still whirling. He rolls his bare limbs luxuriously in the grass, scraping his skin on a thousand grass-blades, in and out of the inky darkness below the tree, excited by his adventure, his nerves, the illicitness of what he has just done. Swimming! At this time of day! At Cuckoo Weir! Strictly out of bounds! Then running naked! Like Achilles!

He rolls deep into the shadow of the tree, rubbing himself hard against the roughness of the ground, taking an imprint of its lumps and hollows on his skin, the prickly acorns, the broken twigs, ecstatic at their jabbing, their abrasive touch. His whole body is on fire. He has never before known such liveness, such jagged penetrations of electric energy, shooting through each nerve, each cell of his body.

The fever is still with him as he stands up. He feels it inside him like a secret knowledge. It will not leave him now. His clothes lie in a heap on a wooden bench by the trunk of the tree. He stops to take a last sigh of freedom, to feel his sacred forbidden nudity sting like sea spray. He surveys the fields, the distant school buildings, their lights glowing along the purple horizon. He reaches for his shirt.

A man's voice, heavy with menace, growls from the shadows.

'What are you doing here, boy?'

A match is struck. It flares over the bowl of a pipe. He sees the strands of tobacco with hallucinatory clarity, lying close-packed, nut-brown, writhing as the flame sears them. Through the twisting veil of smoke he glimpses the melancholy green eyes, the ruddy slab-like cheeks, the vast Roman nose, of his housemaster, Mr Joynes.

'Having a romp, are we?'

'No, sir.'

'What, then?'

'I wanted a swim, sir.'

'There are times and places for swimming.'

'I know, sir.'

'This is a dangerous part of the river. And a damned stupid time to go in. Does anyone know you're here?'

'No sir.'

'Right.' Mr Joynes drew a cane from the depths of his gown. 'There's a cure for this kind of foolery. Hands on the bench, boy.'

The child bent over, gripping the rough-grained planks in his fingers. The cane whistled and struck. A sour, stinging cut like a lightning flash. Heat searing his skin. He held the bench hard. Swish! – the darkness exploded into sparks before his eyes.

'You won't do this again in a hurry,' said Joynes.

'No, sir,' he muttered.

Swish!

'Your father would be most displeased.'

'Yes, sir.'

Swish. Ah, the electric pain!

'It's not easy being a schoolmaster. Hurting when all you mean is kindness and the bringing down of pride.'

Swish.

'But one must be cruel to be kind.'

Swish.

'Spare the rod and ruin the child.'

That was five. He waited for a sixth.

'Ah, we have drawn blood, I see. Stay where you are.'

He felt something touch his buttocks. A brief splash. A silence. The housemaster breathing heavily. A dripping down his legs.

'Don't move. We must wipe that off. That blood...'

The boy waited as Joynes rubbed busily at his bum.

'There we are. Now get dressed and be off with you.'

He stayed where he was, still waiting for the sixth stroke of the cane.

'Stand up boy, it's all done.'

'That's only five, sir.'

'Is it? Then you have got off lightly. But I have put my cane away now and am not inclined to take it out again. Off you go! Quick!'

He stood up, feeling slightly disappointed. He dressed, and

ran stiffly back across the fields to his boarding house.

Such was the start to a richly decadent swimming life. Algernon Charles Swinburne, poet, aesthete, sado-masochist. The eldest son of an admiral, he had loved the water since infancy, when he was 'held up naked in my father's arms and brandished between his hands, then shot like a stone from a sling through the air, shouting and laughing with delight, head foremost into the coming wave.' That early exhilaration, vivid in his memory from summers on the Isle of Wight, was usurped by more complex pleasures. Through the brutality of public school, punishment became an essential element of his emotional life, fused with reward in the steamy laboratory of his imagination. Monstrously charged with nervous energy, he found the excitement and pain of flogging a blessed release of tension. Throughout his adult years, Swinburne sought out violent encounters with rivers and the sea, exposing himself to powerful currents, stormy breakers, rugged coasts of rock and reef, the lash of wind and wave, the scraping and cutting of splintered shells.

The Mediterranean was too placid for his purposes. He preferred the aggression of the English Channel, the North Sea, the Atlantic Ocean. The coast of Cornwall was ideal. One day at Tintagel he risked drowning as the tide raced in, and had to 'run at it and into the water and up or down over some awfully sharp and shell-encrusted rocks which cut my feet to fragments, had twice to plunge again into the sea, which was filling all the coves and swinging and swelling heavily between the rocks; once fell flat in it, and got so thrashed and kicked that I might have been in Denham's clutches. I found a deep cut which was worse than any ever inflicted by a birch.'

Denham is a tutor in Swinburne's novel *Lesbia Brandon*, a tale of frustrated passions – sapphic, incestuous, sadistic –

in which flogging plays the role of a relief valve in a steam engine. Here is Herbert, the hero, enjoying a swim.

'He panted and shouted with pleasure among breakers where he could not stand two minutes the blow of a roller that beat him off his feet and made him laugh and cry out in ecstasy: he rioted in the roaring water like a young sea-beast, sprang at the throat of waves that threw him flat, pressed up against their soft fierce bosoms and fought for their sharp embraces; grappled with them as lover with lover, flung himself upon them with limbs that laboured and yielded deliciously, till the scourging of the surf made him red from the shoulders to the knees, and sent him on shore whipped by the sea into a single blush of the whole skin.'

The complete decadent *plongeur*, Swinburne spent a lifetime seeking to rekindle the intensity of that summer evening on the river bank, an exquisite combination of pleasure and pain, guilt and exuberance, shame and ecstasy. Naked, wet, bloody, humiliated – things could hardly be better. Indeed they could only go downhill from now on. What an example to all aesthetes, perverts, sportsmen and dandies the world over! Here was the philosopher's stone, which transforms the common metal of daily life into gold.

Yet there is more to this strange alchemist's work. A brilliant hoaxer and fantasist, Swinburne liked to reinvent his own life, forging memories and feelings to suit the demands of his desires. He conjured non-existent beings out of thin air: the novelist Ernest Wheldrake, who murdered an infant in order to lend authenticity to one of his descriptions; the French poet Félicien Cossu, whose work, inspired by de Sade (but far more explicit), was so obscene that it could not possibly be quoted in England. These and other creations duped large numbers of people, including professional critics. The recollection of that

Eton punishment, so vivid in Swinburne's mind, was one of these inventions, planted in the garden of his own memory to bear the most exotic of fruit. Inflamed by that hot and nervous disposition, his imagination metamorphosed the mild Mr Joynes into the cruel Mr Denham, a man who liked to flog his pupils in a cloud of incense, or, if he happened to be outdoors, amid the scent of stocks and lilies. And so the decadence was duplicated: its rich sado-masochistic undercurrent driven by a deeper and darker flow of mendacity.

Water – used by the alchemist for *ablution* and *dissolution* – is the great alternative medium of existence. It calls with a siren song, a lure honeyed with enchantment, danger and mystery. Its glugging and lapping recall the music of the absinthe bottle. To the exquisite, bruised soul of the Decadent, water is a place of refuge, of rebirth, of return to the womb and beyond, deep into the oceanic past of reptilian and pisciform days.

As Swinburne put it in 'The Swimmer':

A purer passion, a lordlier leisure,
A peace more happy than lives on land,
Fulfils with pulse of diviner pleasure
The dreaming head and the steering hand...

How true! These words were painted in gold along the rim of the Plunge Pool at our Edinburgh Restaurant, and served as inspiration to many a weary diner, seeking solace from a harsh world.

Decadent swimmers move in ancient waters. The Roman emperor Heliogabalus "would not bathe in any pool unless it was treated with saffron or some other expensive perfume," wrote Aelius Lampridius in the *Augustan History*. Tiberius, says Suetonius, "trained young boys" – whom he called his 'little fishes' – to swim between his legs and lick and nibble him" at his villa in Capri. His contemporary, Herod, King of Judea, was an inveterate builder of swimming-baths – one of his best is an improbable lido in the sky at Masada, hundreds of feet above the desert. This tiered, semi-circular pool, like a submerged Roman theatre, enjoys a vast and desolate panorama of rocky hills. As he swam he could gaze down on the glittering, poisonous wastes of the Dead Sea – the perfect setting for a descent into regal madness and paranoia. One can imagine the old tyrant basking up there like a jewelled shark, hazed, soothing his shot nerves in the cool waters, surveying his kingdom and the immense landscape vanishing away to the east with a strange detachment. Perhaps, in retrospect, he should have spent less time in the swimming pool and more on reputation-management. But he lived as he chose, and paid the price.

A pleasing curiosity of Masada is that it seems, by a trick of perspective, to stand higher than all the surrounding terrain. Yet its cisterns were gravity-fed, charged once a year by flash-floods rushing down riverbeds and aqueducts from the mountains to the west – a deluge that would have given Swinburne the battering of a lifetime.

Diving, like a pearl fisher, into the history of *homo aquaticus,* we find surprising treasures. Akira Kurosawa, the film director, like so many of the world's great aesthetes, came from a military background. His father was an army gymnastics instructor, who taught him the techniques of Samurai swimming. According to this ancient discipline, a well-trained warrior could move swiftly and silently through water of all types – sea, lake, marsh and river – mastering waves, currents, whirlpools, muddy and dark waters, while keeping weapons and headgear dry. He could dive or float, shoot a bow and arrow, fight with a sword or fire a musket while treading water. He could swim in armour, carry heavy weights, cover long distances. He could propel himself through the water with his hands and feet tied. He knew life-saving, resuscitation, swimming medicine and history. He displayed good manners (how to salute a lord from a floating position), and had mastered such ornamental accomplishments as calligraphy and holding a paper fan between his toes while swimming. Each technique was associated with a spiritual quality:

diving for bravery
submersion for patience
floating for serene mind
swimming against currents for a combative spirit
long-distance swimming for will-power
cold water swimming for perseverance
life-saving for benevolence
the study of history and etiquette for respect and caution.

The young Kurosawa made good use of his skills. He dived into a treacherous whirlpool in the local river, keen to satisfy his curiosity about what lay at the bottom. His village friends tried to stop him, and insisted on making a rope of their sashes so as to pull him out in case of trouble. Confidently, he dived in. As part of his training in the Kankairyu style he had learned to swim safely under a large cargo junk. Reaching the midpoint of the ship, he had been sucked against its bottom, but following his teacher's instructions, he turned over, pushed off with his arms and legs, and swam on. 'Since I had had this experience with a junk,' he wrote, 'a mere whirlpool seemed like nothing to me.' He quickly found himself pinned to the bottom of the river. Telling himself not to panic, he tried to crawl downstream, away from the whirlpool. But the boys on the bank were hauling on the rope. He could make no progress. Now he did panic. 'I had no choice but to try crawling in the direction from which I was being pulled by the waist, against the current. After what seemed like hours of extreme pain and abject terror, I began to float towards the surface. I kicked my feet and shot out of the water.'

His friends were astonished. Kurosawa came to regard this adventure, and other aquatic exploits, as a form of rebirth, a voyage into the unconscious, penetrating the mythic hinterland of the Japanese soul. Like an Arthurian knight wandering through ancient forests in search of the Holy Grail, or Marlow chugging up the Congo in *Heart of Darkness*, he followed a physical path into a spiritual landscape.

Kurosawa's compatriot, Yukio Mishima, used water in a more contorted way. As a boy he spent time by the seaside guiltily admiring the well-hung swimmers as they emerged from the waves. Then he visited Greece and was overwhelmed by the manly beauty of classical statues in the 'copious, virulent light' at the Delphi museum. He realised that he had lived in the grip of a dark, morbid form of intellectual overdevelopment, ignoring the body and the senses. Suddenly he found 'a will to health in the Nietzschean sense' and determined to 'learn the language of the flesh, much as one would learn a foreign language'. He became an obsessive bodybuilder and sun-worshipper, cultivating muscular strength and grace, practising *kendo*, and learning to swim. Combined with his fascination for gladiators, Japanese warriors and the piercings of Saint

Sebastian, he began the ascent towards apotheosis. In the last summer of his life, he worked out punishingly and swam twice a day, wearing black cotton briefs with brass buckles, sculpting his flesh to complete the transformation from man of words into man of action and muscle. An heroic end, he believed, should have 'a strictly classical body as its vehicle'. On 25 November 1970 he attempted a *coup d'état*, failed, and committed ritual suicide by *seppuku,* turning a sharp knife on his belly and slicing laterally; the act was completed, in the traditional way, by an assistant cutting off his head.

Mishima is a source of inspiration to us. A Samurai Narcissus of impeccable credentials, he stands as a beacon to his ideal of the 'sword and chrysanthemum' – warrior and writer. While our ideal is slightly less military (we prefer the dildo and the perfume bottle), we acknowledge dear Yukio, by mesmeric congruence, as a kindred spirit. We often read to each other from his bodybuilding masterpiece, *Sun and Steel,* a form of mental exercise every bit as invigorating as a two-hour work-out in the gym – and not nearly so tedious.

Our Caribbean exile has drawn us to the sea in ways we never imagined. When we resided in Edinburgh, the sight of a wind-scoured Firth of Forth, traversed by that hideous iron bridge, navigated by nuclear submarines, cement barges, plastic cider bottles, shopping bags, driftwood and mutant catfish, would regularly send shivers of revulsion through our nervous systems. Havana is a different story. The Playas de Este are our afternoon playground. We love their palette of turquoise waves, hot white sand and salt-spangled black bodies. We are well-known figures along this coast, especially at El Chivo and Mi Cayito, with our yellow Harley Davidson and blue picnic basket. Even the police have become our friends.

Inspired by this maritime life, driven on by an unstoppable curiosity about the sea's otherworld, we have embarked on a series of experimental journeys. These began with a scuba-diving course, which Durian allowed himself to be talked into by a honey-tongued young *pinguero* called Sammy. To prevent jealous scenes of the kind he had provoked in St Petersburg, when he sloped off with a *danseuse* from the Kirov Ballet for a weekend of endoscopy in Akademgorodok, Durian signed us both in for the lessons. It was a shrewd move. Our days among the coral reefs opened up a new cosmos, as lonely, mysterious and uncanny as outer space. A sense of wonder seemed to ripple through us continuously in those weightless, peacock days.

Although he did not admit it at the time, Durian was not in fact a diving virgin. He confessed one evening that he had 'tasted these pleasures before.' By way of explanation he produced one of the hermetically numbered notebooks that contain his memoirs...

In September 1992 I was contacted by my friend Oliver Crompton-March, asking if I would like to join him in Sinai for the shooting of a film. It was loosely based on a short story I had written about a swimmer masturbating a mermaid, and he said he would value my input.

Oliver was an old family friend. A notorious bisexual of the post-War years, he had moved from London to Cairo in 1947 in search of sexual apotheosis. He must have found what he wanted, as he stayed there for the next half-century. He also found a career there – thanks to a pair of chance encounters.

The first was with Hector Lucan, visiting from Benghazi with his American wife, Cecile. Hector Lucan is generally regarded as the 'Father of Aero-erotica', a highly specialised branch of the film industry which flourished and died with him. Cecile, who had starred in so many of Hector's high-flying films, undoubtedly beguiled Oliver despite the fact that she was no longer in her prime. The younger man no doubt envied the older and longed to emulate or outdo him.

The second fortuitous meeting was with Hans Schlemeier, the Viennese pioneer of underwater documentaries. The Austrian took Oliver on diving expeditions to the Red Sea at the southern tip of the Sinai peninsula, where today stands that grotesque monument to vulgarity, Sharm el-Sheikh. (This Egyptian holiday resort has all the subtlety and elegance of a Russian gangster in a shellsuit. When I heard in 2005 that the place had been the target of bombings I assumed quite naturally that it was the work of enraged aesthetes.)

When Hans and Oliver began diving in the waters of the Red Sea, the desert landscape was still one of biblical purity. What the young English bisexual saw here was the possibility of exploiting the ocean in the same way that Hector Lucan had exploited the pornographic potential of the skies. For Oliver, there was something inherently erotic about water. He realised that as a film studio the sea beneath the waves presented significant advantages. The pellucid blue water provided the most enchanting lighting effects and the warm temperatures would not adversely effect the performance of his male actors. Brilliantly-coloured fish would act as a shifting backdrop to the erotic scenes. The framing of a shot might contain both the phallic conger eel and the vaginal undulations of the clam. It was also an impossible space for the authorities to police effectively.

Oliver duly set up C-M Productions and it is generally accepted that within this small niche of the film world, he created some masterpieces, most notably his 1948 Breathless in Rubber, *and* Going Down! *(1950).*

Before I set off for Sinai, I was told that I would need a wetsuit. I at once made for Westmacott and Green, my tailor in Jermyn Street, for a fitting. Both Mr W and Mr G admitted that they had never received such a request before, but they would 'do their utmost to fulfil Mr Gray's desires'. Within two weeks I was being helped into my brusquely constrictive black pinstripe wetsuit. To complete the outfit, I had commissioned a neoprene bowler hat with attached diving mask. In the ensemble I resembled a large and very expensive dildo.

A week later I arrived at Oliver's camp on the shores of the Red Sea. Squinting through the shimmering heat of the Sinai desert I could make out rusting Egyptian weaponry lying half-buried in the sand. Oliver greeted me like a long-lost son. He had aged considerably but still retained a spriteliness which I put down to the constant companionship of the Arab boys who attended to his every need. My training began immediately. Over mint juleps, Oliver gave me a vivid and detailed account of the various ways in which I could die or go insane under water. I was now ready for my first open water dive. The following day, we set out on his sailing yacht Aurora; *myself, Oliver and his two performers. Both were unutterably beautiful and rendered even more so by the weightlessness of their bodies as they slid into the water. Neither of them was constrained by the cumbersome equipment that Oliver and I were wearing.*

> *They were freediving, taking lungfuls of oxygen from bottles on the seabed and then holding their breath for considerable periods of time. What Oliver was seeking to combine was filming the equivalent of auto-asphyxiation with underwater copulation. Much of the excitement of such films was generated through the possibility that if anything went wrong the actors might not make it to the surface in time.*
>
> *At the end of a full day's filming we returned to the yacht and later that evening Oliver showed me the rushes. The footage was strange and beautiful, with some extraordinary close-ups on the faces of the lovers as they reached the very limits of their oxygen supply, their eyes bulging while still locked in sexual congress. A final shot in the shifting aquatic light has the male lead ejaculating into the water as his female companion plays with the string of semen like a necklace.*

Nothing in our Havana diving lessons quite matched up to those scenes under the Red Sea, but they were nonetheless a revelation. And our underwater experiences soon led us to a new obsession, with a particularly unlikely class of sea beast: the squid.

It is hard to say quite how or why this obsession began. There are more immediately attractive fish in the ocean, but somehow the three hundred species of squid spoke to us. There is so much that is appealing in the squid – their creamy, scrotum-like mantles stippled with purple, their huge, melancholy, death-dealing eyes, their jet propulsion systems and prehensile tentacles – some armed with tiny teeth! They are like aquatic Chinese lanterns, freaked with lurid colours, wobbling along on wings of rubber and silk through the twilight kingdoms of Neptune.

The literature of the squid is limited but very fine. Here are the immortal words of Zbigniew L. Sbrzisczek's *Anatomy of a Cephalopod*: "In transparent young, five or six millimetres long, the rectal valves can be seen beating downward into the anus. As they descend the anal lips open; as they rise the anal lips close. This action forces water into the rectum... Contractions of the rectum force the water out through the anus..." Does this not conjure up the most exquisite visions? There is nothing remotely similar to be found in Dante or Shakespeare.

But the heart of our fascination lies in a pear-shaped organ situated above the rectum – the ink sac. Its primary use is for defence. A quick puff from the inky reservoir, and the water turns as black as a panther's arse. Disorienting and suffocating, it allows Mr Squid to spirit himself away in a cloud of unknowing to safer waters.

We see a stranger use for that silvery little bladder. Extracting the fluid with a scalpel, we mix it with the pressings of purple figs, molasses, grape must, balsamic vinegar, psilocybin mushrooms, tincture of stag's horn, poppy seeds, black sesame, prune schnapps, London porter and dried blood – a liquid counterpart of the dark matter of the universe. I once took a monster dose of this cocktail before an invited audience in Zurich, and was subject to some remarkable hallucinations. These I attempted to record, in the midst of my convulsions, by scribbling on sheets of cartridge paper with a wax crayon. The writings turned out to be gibberish, but the experiment was hailed by a group of Russian scientists as a breakthrough, revealing, as they put it, 'the curious contents of Mr Lucan's subconscious and the power of certain alkaloids to alter the wavelength of electro-magnetic radiation in the brain'.

THE DECADENT SPORTSMAN

Further aquatic epiphanies were visited on us during our travels with the Hell Fire Touring Club. Our friend Paul Renner took us to visit the monastery of Kremsmünster in Upper Austria, where the monks had constructed a series of fish-ponds in a cloister ornamented with tritons, fountains and arcades. Here they bred carp, sturgeon and trout for their refectory tables. In three of the pools the fish swam or lingered randomly, suspended like plump pickled fruit, or, with the occasional flick of a tail, flitting to left or right as the whim took them. In the fourth pool, an inscrutable collective purpose had seized the entire population. A shoal of young trout were swimming in an energetic circle, hurriedly, as if pressed for time. We waited for the rotation to stop, yet it never faltered. Like the movement of a clock the fish circled constantly, a glinting silver machine of muscles, blood and fins. Yet they moved anti-clockwise, swimming against the current of time.

As we contemplated this *perpetuum mobile*, Renner reminded us that not far from there lived a man – perhaps the only man in history – capable of conceiving and building such a mechanism: August Strindberg. Alchemist, playwright, madman and genius, he lodged for a while at Dornach-im-Strudengau, overlooking a bend in the Danube where the waters twist into vicious whirlpools, vortices of death for sailors and swimmers, fountains of gold for the local pilots and guides. The great man's spirit seemed to roam this cloister, his voice whispering feverishly among the gloomy arcades.

Dreams, hallucinations, fantasies – these are utterly real to me. If my pillow takes on a human shape, I believe that shape exists. And if anyone says it is only my imagination, I reply: "Only? What my inner eye sees means a great deal to me! My pillow is made of birds' feathers and linen. These once carried the force of life in their fibres. What I see in them is soul, the power to create forms, and it is certainly real, since I can draw these images and show them to others."

Sometimes I hear voices in the water-pipes, like the echo of fishes conversing in distant oceans. If we could harness their electrical energy, what mechanisms we could propel! Machines for weather-prediction, the measurement of celestial time, even furnaces for refining gold... Do not tell me this is not possible!

We gazed down again at the pond. The hundreds of fish had become one fish, each body a scale on one giant body, a collective soul threading the centuries, whirled in the vast spiral nebula of sidereal time. As the fins of the clock moved backwards, revisiting each moment the place they had just left, they inexorably revealed the signature of their creator, who had poured years of contorted mental energy into his search for the Molecule of Gold. And to what end?

I am not seeking gold. I have found it. Having found it, I have given it away. Once there is a means of manufacturing gold cheaply, its monetary value will be zero.

Decadent swimming is a visionary activity. Writing of the Romantic poets, Charles Sprawson says "[they] experienced through their swims the classic constituents of an opium dream: 'the feeling of blissful buoyancy, the extension of time, contrasts of temperature, the bliss of the outcast'." He clearly shares these feelings himself. "Anyone who submerges some way below the surface into deep water," he writes, "can experience those nightmare visions of de Quincey's, inspired by drugs and the prison etchings of Piranesi, of sinking down through huge vaulted airless spaces, among rocks and columns that rise up from the ocean floor in a limitless and yet claustrophobic expansion of space, alone, but not unobserved; there is a sense that one is always under surveillance, invisible enemies and predators are somewhere hidden beyond in the shadowy gloom and remote recesses; the sensibility sharpens; the slightest touch or sound can cause alarm in this silent world."

Roger Deakin has his own definition. "When you enter the water, something like metamorphosis happens. Leaving behind the land, you go through the looking-glass surface and enter a new world... You see and experience things when you're swimming in a way that is completely different from any other. You are *in* nature, part and parcel of it, in a far more complete and intense way than on dry land, and your sense of the present is overwhelming." Swimming in natural water, he adds, is both healing and subversive, allowing us to "regain a sense of what is old and wild in these islands, by getting off the beaten track and breaking free of the official version of things."

Llewellyn Powys believed there is an 'ichthyosaurus ego' sunk deep inside us, with which swimmers in remote places make contact, helping them to resist the vulgarities and indifference of contemporary life, and to rediscover what civilisation has lost.

There is also a strong erotic urge in swimming. Paul Valéry spoke of *fornication avec l'onde*, Flaubert of the sea's 'thousand liquid nipples travelling all over the body'. Our old friend Huysmans was hugely excited by the sight of Hokusai's

Diving Girl and Octopuses: 'it depicts a Japanese woman mounted by an octopus; with its tentacles the horrible beast sucks the tips of her breasts and rummages in her mouth, while its head drinks from her lower parts. The almost superhuman expression of agony and sorrow, which convulses this long, graceful human figure with aquiline nose, and the hysterical joy which emanates at the same time from her forehead, from those eyes closed as if in death, are admirable.'

Isidore Ducasse, *alias* the Comte de Lautréamont, *alias* 'the Montevidean', pushed things a little further in *Les Chants de Maldoror*, where the hero, enjoying a tempest by the seashore, watches a ship foundering in high seas:

Standing on a rock, the wind lashing my cloak and hair, I gazed in ecstasy as the force of the storm hurled itself at a ship, under a starless sky. Triumphantly I watched all the episodes of this drama, from the moment when the ship dropped its anchors to the moment when it sank, a fatal garment that dragged down all those whom it enfolded, like a mantle, into the bowels of the sea. But the moment was approaching when I too would become an actor in these scenes of natural chaos. When the place of combat clearly showed that the ship had gone to spend the rest of its days in the basement of the sea, a number of the people who had been sucked by the waves began to reappear on the surface. They grasped each other, in twos and threes; the perfect way to lose their lives; for they encumbered each other's movements and sank like holed pots... What is this army of sea monsters that cuts so swiftly through the waves? There are six of them; their fins are powerful, they carve a passage through the mountainous seas. Of all these humans, waving their four limbs in this unstable continent, the sharks soon make an omelette without eggs, sharing the spoils according to the law of the strongest. Blood mingles with water, water with blood. Their ferocious eyes light the scene of carnage... But what is that tumult, down there, on the horizon? It looks like a water spout. What lusty strokes! I see what it is. An enormous female shark has come to take her share of the duck liver pâté and cold boiled beef. She is furious; for she arrives hungry. A fight begins between her and the other sharks, as they dispute the few palpitating limbs that float here and there, without saying a word, on the surface of the scarlet cream. Right and left she snaps with her teeth, dealing mortal wounds. But three surviving sharks still encircle her, and she is forced to turn in every direction to outmanoeuvre them. With growing emotion, unknown before now, the spectator on the shore follows this new style of naval battle. His eyes are fixed on this brave female with her mighty teeth. He hesitates no more, he shoulders his rifle, and, with his habitual skill, lodges his second bullet in the ear of one of the male sharks, as he appears momentarily above a wave. Two males remain, their rage greater than ever. From the top of the rock, the man, with the taste of brine in his mouth, throws himself into the sea and swims towards the pleasantly coloured carpet, holding in his hand the steel-bladed knife that he always keeps with him. Now each male shark is faced with just one enemy. He advances on his weary adversary, and, taking his time, plunges the sharp blade into its belly. The mobile citadel deals easily with the last enemy... The swimmer and the female shark he has saved are now alone. They look into each other's eyes for a few minutes, each astonished to see such ferocity in the other's stare. They circle, keeping each other in sight, thinking: "I was wrong; here is someone meaner." Then, with a common accord, between two waves, they slide towards each other, with mutual admiration, the female shark parting the waters with her fins, Maldoror beating the waves with his arms: and hold their breath, in deep veneration, each yearning to gaze, for the first time, on their living likeness. When they are three metres apart, making no effort, they fall suddenly together, like lovers, and embrace each other with dignity and gratitude, in a clasp as tender as that between a brother and his sister. Carnal desires are swift to follow this show of friendship. Two nervous thighs glue themselves fast to the monster's clammy skin, like two leeches; and, with arms and fins entwined around the body of the object of their desire, enveloped with love, while their throats and breasts soon make a single glaucous mass, panting with seaweed-breath; in the midst of the storm that continues to rage; while the lightning flashes; with the foaming wave as a marriage-bed, cradled by an ocean current, and rolling around themselves, towards the depths of the abyss, they join in a long, chaste, hideous coupling!... At last, I had found someone like myself!... I was no longer alone in this life!... Our thoughts were so similar!... This was my first love!

Here at last is a worthy companion to Algernon Swinburne! Few have followed where these two pioneers have led. Ducasse himself quailed at the extremity of his achievement, deciding after *Maldoror* that the mapping of evil must now be followed by quieter and more wholesome pursuits.

Yet there is one further step to be taken.

We have enjoyed many visionary immersions, both real and imagined. We come now to a third, and certainly the finest, form of swimming – the impossible swim. This, combined with a determination to attempt it, constitutes a unique aesthetic act. The great Captain Webb, first swimmer of the English Channel, drowned as he tried to shoot the rapids below the Niagara Falls. Edward Trelawney survived them, although he scarcely knew how:

> *I now remembered the terrible whirlpool below me, I could make no progress, the stream was mastering me. I seemed to be held by the legs and sucked downwards, the scrumming surf broke over and blinded me, I began to ship water. In the part of the river I had now drifted to the water was frightfully agitated, it was broken and raging all around me. Why did I attempt to cross a part of the river that none had ever crossed before? I heard the voices of the dead calling to me. I actually thought, as my mind grew darker, that they were tugging at my feet...*

He was lucky enough to be spun out of the vortex and went floating towards the shore:

> *I heard the boiling commotion of the tremendous Rapids and saw the spume flying in the air a little below me, and then I lay stranded, sick and dizzy, everything still seemed whirling round and round and the waters singing in my ears.* [Then came the realisation that, at the age of 41, he was past his physical peak.] *My*

shadow trembling on the black rock as reflected by the last rays of the setting sun shows me as in a glass, that my youth and strength have fled.

In the 1950s Patrick Leigh Fermor dived from a Greek fishing boat off Cape Taenarus at the southern tip of the Peloponnese and tried to swim into the mouth of the ancient underworld. Despite the improbability of the scheme, his description of the flooded sea-cave, sparkling like a crystal with refracted blue light, is one of the high points of his book *Mani.* Of course he failed to find the fabled portal, with its downward sloping road to the kingdom of Hades, but his immersion in the icy water, contrasting with the fierce summer's heat outside, transmits an authentic frisson to the reader, no matter how deep his leather armchair, how bright his log fire, how strong his whisky and soda.

Leigh Fermor's friend Kevin Andrews, author of another excellent memoir, *The Flight of Ikaros,* unintentionally found an entrance to the underworld just a few miles away, in the strait between the port of Kapsali, in southern Kythera, and the strange cone of rock named Hytra ('Cauldron') that emerges powerfully from the sea a couple of thousand yards offshore. Attempting to make the crossing there, he was drowned in a sudden storm in 1989.

Our favourite impossible swim is described by Roger Deakin in his book *Waterlog.* Deciding to follow the protagonist in John Cheever's short story *The Swimmer,* as well as his totemic ancestors the otter and the eel ('swimmers who often cross country by land, following their own instinctive maps'), he sets out from his moated grange in Suffolk to swim across Britain in every conceivable form of water: chalk streams, rivers, drains, canals, estuaries, lakes, ponds, lagoons, flooded caves, seas, and – boldest of all – municipal swimming baths. In the Map Room at Cambridge University Library he studies a nautical chart of the Gulf of Corryvreckan, off the west coast of Scotland:

I pored over the six-inch map, staring at the single word 'whirlpool' marked in the almost mile-wide straits that separate Jura from the rugged uninhabited island of Scarba. I calculated the exact distance across at the narrowest point: 1,466 yards. Practically speaking, the distance was meaningless, because the tidal currents would carry a swimmer well off the course of a straight line. I felt sure that, in the right conditions and at the right moment in the complex pattern of the tides, I had a chance of pulling off the Corryvreckan swim. I knew, at any rate, that I would have to go up there and try.

Many months later, he reaches Jura, and pitches his tent in the lonely hills among swarms of midges. He recalls a young man named Bill Dunn, who came to help George Orwell run a farm on Jura in the late 1940s. Dunn had lost a leg in the war, and used a wooden one. He took this off before smearing himself in sheep's fat and setting out across the strait. The sea was flat and calm, and it took him about half an hour. Deakin lies in his tent thinking of Dunn, full of apprehension about the next day: 'I dreamed comprehensively of the Corryvreckan all night.'

The morning began unexpectedly grey, with a sprinkling of fine rain driving in off the sea as I set off up the last two miles of dilapidated path to the gulf itself. Obeying some inescapable impulse to confront my nocturnal fear, I trudged on north like a lemming. There was no telling which of us was in greater turmoil: myself or the whirlpool. I heard the commotion of water before I saw it, a low-pitched, continuous seething of brawling waves. The unnerving sound carried vividly on the damp drizzle. These were not the wide blue skies I had imagined; the scene before me was mostly muted shades of grey. The shore was a fortified steep escarpment, with no beaches, only fissured rock, indented by narrow clefts, alternately filled and sucked dry by the Atlantic swell with the awful gurgling I associate with the dentist's chair. This was it. The Gulf of Corryvreckan. One of the most notorious stretches of water anywhere around the British Isles. Standing before it, at the extremity of the island, I felt like The Last Man in Europe, *Orwell's original working title for* Nineteen Eighty-Four.

The sea all round this part of the Western Isles is so full of warring tide-rips, sluicing through narrow gaps between islands in deep channels, that it is rarely still. Enormous volumes of water have to find their way in and out of the islands that stand in their way. So serious is the danger of the Gulf of Corryvreckan that it is officially classed by the Royal Navy as 'unnavigable'. It is not much over half a mile wide, yet it is more than 300 feet deep over most of its width, except in one significant spot, where a huge conical rock is sunk only ninety feet below the surface. It is called Cailleach, 'The Hag'. The special menace of the Corryvreckan is created by the sheer force of the Atlantic tidal wave, which sometimes races through the passage at the rate of fifteen knots. The effect of the pyramidal rock is to create a standing wave up to thirty feet high which combines with a welter of eddying turbulence along both shores to create the

Corryvreckan whirlpool.

What no navigation guide could communicate is the deeply unsettling atmosphere of the place, the intense physical presence of the whirlpool and the scale of the turbulence. Wind and tide were herding the waves into the narrow gulf, and they stretched away, falling over themselves, for a mile across the sea beyond the outer coast of Scarba.

The whirlpool was clearly visible, three hundred yards offshore towards the western end of the gulf. Inside its circumference was a mêlée of struggling white breakers, charging about in every direction, head-butting one another. Outside, the surface was deadly smooth. The neatly-folded swimming trunks in my rucksack felt somehow irrelevant as I stood by the shore, feeling a very tiny figure, unable to take my eyes from the epicentre of the vortex. It seemed scarcely credible that a swimmer could have made this crossing from Jura to Scarba.

To distract the reader, and no doubt himself too, from the appalling prospect of plunging into this maelstrom, Deakin recounts the tale of Breachan, the love-struck Norse king whose ship was swallowed up in the gulf: hence the name, Coire Breachain. The king's body was pulled from the shore by his faithful black dog, and buried in a cave a mile along the coast.

To avoid a similar fate, Deakin accepts the inevitable: 'I had to face the fact that I wasn't going to swim the Corryvreckan, at least not on this occasion. It would be madness to swim alone, and suicidal in these conditions.' With a final salute to the gulf's 'excess of mad energy', which he would like, on a calmer day, to attempt once more to come close to – 'like tiptoeing past a sleeping tiger' – he at last abandons the scene: 'Only the deer saw me turn away from the Corryvreckan and make my way slowly back up the hillside.'

In shirking this challenge, Deakin displays the level of courage and dedication required to become a truly Decadent sportsman.

3

THE DUELLIST

'The problem with sport these days, my boy, is the lack of fatalities.'

I still have a clear recollection of these words uttered by my father, Col. Pelham Gray of the Queen's 17th Artificers. I must have been about six years old at the time. We were at Laingstons, the family home, sitting together in the orangery where he was teaching me to play lightning chess. He had convinced me that the chess clock was wired up to a small explosive device and that if I did not make a correct move and hit the button on the clock within 20 seconds we would both of us be blown to pieces. This singular coaching technique was only to be expected from a man who was one of the most notorious mercenaries of his generation. Hence his impatience with any sporting contest in which the loser or losers survived. He was of the opinion that death was the only adequate response to the ignominy of defeat. Even now I cannot catch sight of a chess board without trembling violently and wanting to vomit.

Papa was right of course. There are precious few fatalities, and sport is immeasurably poorer for it. Gone are the days when the Aztec ball court at Tenochtitlan resounded to the roars of the spectators from behind racks adorned with the skulls of sacrificial victims. It has long been assumed that the skulls were those of the losers, although, given that sacrifice to Huitzilpochtli was an honour, it may well have been the victors who were eviscerated, beheaded and put on display.

An indication of the depressingly low number of sportsmen killed in action can be gathered from the fact that when a death does occur, it is highly newsworthy. Among the better-known in the roll call are Tommy Simpson, the Tour de France rider whose amphetamine-and alcohol-ravaged body ground to a permanent halt on his suicidal ascent of the Col de Ventoux in 1965, and Vladimir Smirnov, who died during the 1982 World Fencing Championships in Rome: his opponent's foil snapped in a lunge and the jagged end penetrated Smirnov's mask, pierced an eye and lodged in his brain. In fact he was kept on a life-support machine until after the final touch of the final event so that it could not be said that he died during the championships – an exquisite piece of news management! More recently, the Gabon Powerboat Grand Prix claimed a victim in William Nocker of Tiverton. Returning to the sport after a five-year ban for adding water to a rival's fuel supply, this distinguished sportsman flipped his boat at 120 mph, a manoeuvre which few survive.

Most newsworthy of all was Ayrton Senna, the Brazilian god of speed, whose death drove his fans to despair. Their tributes are published on a memorial internet site where the intensity of the grief is matched only by the wondrous banality of its expression:

> *Ever since his death, every time his name is mentioned or I remember his face, I just go numb and a sadness fills me, like a shadow of darkness creeping across my soul.*

Occasionally these tributes rise, like drugged trout, to the level of doggerel...

*Blurring green, blue and yellow,
Never turned at Tamburello,
Formula One's saddest ever day,
Saw The Greatest Ever taken away.*

What does one weep for first: the death of Senna, or the abysmally low standard of public taste?

With regard to the lack of sporting fatalities, bullfighting remains an honourable exception. Pope Pius V tried to spoil everybody's fun in 1567 by proscribing the corrida with a papal bull, *De Salute Gregis*. Mercifully, this was revoked by his successor, Gregory XIII. And to this day, the highpoint of the bullfighting season remains that glorious moment when a matador sacrifices his life for his sport; that moment when triumph turns to horror; when the crowd in its heart realises it is has played its part, not in the butchering of a dumb brute, but in the death of beauty most elegantly attired in a suit of lights. On August 30th 1985 in the Plaza de Colmenar Viejo, José Cubero Sánchez, 'El Yiyo', had just mortally wounded his bull and was walking away to acknowledge the rapture of the crowd when, with supreme effort, the dying creature knocked him to the ground and gored the matador in the heart. The bull, wanting to toss El Yiyo, could only lift him to his feet and walk him a few steps across the bloody sand of the arena, as if the bull itself were holding up its prize for the appreciation of the crowd. And were there not some in the crowd who at that moment hailed the beast for guaranteeing the truth of the event, for showing that the crudest violence *can* vanquish subtlety and wit and skill?

The last vestige of a sport where the overt intention was

to bring about the death of your opponent was the duelling pistol event, held at two Olympic Games, one in 1906 (at the Intercalated Games which were not officially recognised by the International Olympic Committee) and the other in 1912. The contest required competitors to shoot at mannequins dressed in frock coats. There was a bull's eye painted on the dummy's throat, like the most unfortunate of birthmarks. The mannequin was placed at two distances from the competitor: 20 metres and 30 metres.

Prior to this of course, duelling was one of Europe's most popular pastimes. Can it properly be called a sport? No reason why not. As Mr William Shankley, Liverpool FC's legendary manager, is often misquoted as saying: "Football is not a matter of life and death. It's more important than that". The extraordinary characteristic of the duel, one which makes it arguably the quintessential Decadent sport, is that what prompted it was rarely a matter of life and death. It was considerably *less* important than that, while at the same time the outcome of the duel itself was literally a matter of life and death. The elegance of so many of the greatest duels was their sheer pointlessness. Edmond de Goncourt tells of a French aristocrat and dandy who was so absurdly oversensitive to any questioning of a woman's honour that he even fought a duel on behalf of the Virgin Mary. On another occasion, upon hearing some wealthy old man railing against the sexual promiscuity and infidelity of his wife, the dandy called the old man out with the words. "How dare you, Sir, speak of my mistress in this way!"

One of the most famous duels of 18th century France took place between the Comte d'Artois and the Duc de Bourbon. At a masked ball on Shrove Tuesday, 1778, the Duchesse de Bourbon spotted the Comte d'Artois, to whom she was undoubtedly attracted, with a certain Mme de Carillac on his arm, who happened to be the ex-mistress of her husband, the duc, whom she, Mme de Carillac, had recently abandoned in favour of the comte. The Duchesse de Bourbon, pursued the comte and Mme de Carillac relentlessly until he, in exasperation and in trying to prevent the duchesse from removing his mask, pressed her mask violently onto her face. The duchesse was hell-bent on revenge for this insult, and despite the king's disapproval, the duc and comte met to settle the *affaire*. The ensuing duel between them was a desultory business. The nobles exchanged a few limp-wristed thrusts devoid of serious intent before falling into each other's arms in reconciliation. Many subsequent commentators were rightly shocked by the whole sorry history, and took this duel to be emblematic of the moral decline of the period. One 19th century historian spluttered: 'A woman of the highest rank insults another woman who had been her husband's mistress; not on that account, but for having become the mistress of another man, to whom she herself was attached; and the foolish husband is made to peril life and liberty by fighting the real object of the dispute who had so far lost sight of all gentlemanly deportment as to insult a female by actually inflicting a blow.'

At the opposite end of the scale from the effete duo described above was the Chevalier d'Andrieux who, during the reign of Louis XIII, had a fearsome reputation. In the course of one duel, his opponent boasted that the chevalier would be his tenth victim. In response, the chevalier pointed out that he would be his seventy second. And he was as good as his word. The 'killer instinct', which is so often alluded to among modern sportsmen, was something the chevalier possessed in spades, and he took it to new heights, or depths. He would often offer to spare the life of a defeated opponent provided he denied God. Those who did so promptly had their throats slit, thus giving the chevalier the pleasure of killing their souls as well as their bodies.

Should one spare the life of a defeated adversary in a gesture of magnanimity? Or go through with what may amount to a cold-blooded execution? This has always been a delicate moral issue. Brantôme, writing in the late 16th century mentions the Italians who were:

> *...rather more cool and deliberate in this business than we are, and somewhat more cruel. In their teaching they have given those who feel disposed to spare their adversary's life the glorious opportunity of showing their generosity by maiming their fallen foe, both in his legs and arms, and moreover giving him a fearful cut across the nose and face, to remind him of their condescension and humanity.*

Certainly the 19th century Irish 'code duello' is clear on this point. Rule 12 states unequivocally:

> *No dumb firing or firing in the air is admissible in any case. The challenger ought not to have challenged without offence, and the challenged ought, if he gave offence, to have made an apology before he came on the ground; therefore children's play must be dishonourable on one side or the other, and is accordingly prohibited.*

To refer to this as a 'rule' understates how seriously the codification of duelling was taken. In Galway, the code was known as the 26 Commandments; they are Jesuitical in their obscurity and subtlety. The first commandment states that:

THE DECADENT SPORTSMAN

The first offence requires the first apology, although the retort may have been more offensive than the insult. Example: A tells B he is impertinent, etc. B retorts that he lies; yet A must make the first apology, because he gave the first offence, and (after one fire) B may explain away the retort by subsequent apology.

And the eleventh commandment would require a roomful of scholastics to unpick its meaning:

Offences originating or accruing from the support of ladies' reputations to be considered as less unjustifiable than any others of the same class, and as admitting of slighter apologies by the aggressor. This is to be determined by the circumstances of the case, but always favourably to the lady.

Let us now consider the process of the duel, where it starts, how it proceeds and how it ends.

The first step is always the insult. In more civilised times, when to live dishonoured was worse than death, and gentlemen were, as Charles Moore puts it, '...in the habit of paying a scrupulous attention to all the supercilious dictates of a captious honour', the insult could be relatively trivial. One did not have to go to the extremes of, say, Lagarde Vallon who liked to induce a duel with written challenges such as: 'I have reduced your house to ashes, ravished your wife, and hanged your children; and now I have the honour to be your mortal enemy, Lagarde.' Needless to say, this level of hyperbole was not required to provoke Lagarde himself. An equally bumptious duellist, Barbanez, sent him a hat decorated with feathers and a note saying that if he wore it in public he risked losing his life. The notorious and bloody 'duel of the hat' resulted in Lagarde stabbing Barbanez three times, once for the hat, once for the feathers and once for the tassel. With supreme effort Lagarde's opponent brought him down and stabbed him fourteen times from his neck to his waist saying: 'I am giving you a scarf to wear with the hat'. By now both men had lost so much blood they collapsed and were carried off, although both miraculously survived their wounds.

In terms of the level of insult necessary, the Comte de Tilly, writing in the late 18th century, gives a fine account of what it took to provoke a duel in France, the birthplace of duelling:

You have had a discussion with a close friend; although it may have exceeded the limits of an excusable warmth, women have observed in it injurious shades; and you would rather expose yourself to kill your friend or be killed by him, than to the mere suspicion on the part of a woman of being deficient in courage.

At a gaming table a misunderstanding arises; a bystander has smiled ironically; he has whispered to his sister, who has whispered something to her cousin: get yourself killed by all means, for you may have been suspected of cheating at play; and nothing can set such a question in a proper light but the thrust of a sword!

Your wife is an acknowledged coquette; get yourself run through the body by her lover, and her honour will be restored. You yourself may have seduced the wife of an honest man, who dares to suspect you, and receives you with ill-humour; kill him; for, having deprived him of happiness and peace, you need not be punctilious about ridding him of life!

The theatre was a particularly good place to find cause for a duel. The notorious Gilbert Rosière, one of New Orleans' finest swordsmen, was described as '...passionately fond of music and nervously sensitive to its melting impressions.' A great frequenter of the opera, his superb head could be seen almost every night towering above the others in the parquette. On one occasion, deeply touched by the pathos of a well-sung *cantilena*, he wept audibly. An imprudent neighbour laughed, but his amusement was of short duration, for no sooner had Rosière noticed the mirth than his tenderness turned to anger.

"C'est vrai," he said. *"Je pleure, mais je donne aussi des calottes."*

By this time the man's face had been slapped and the following day a flesh wound had taught him to be more careful about whom he laughed at.

The Marquis de Tenteniac already had a reputation as one of the most truculent duellists of 18th century France, when, at the theatre one evening, he moved so far onto the stage to witness the drama that the audience began barracking him. In response the Marquis stepped forward and addressed the entire assembly with the words, "Ladies and Gentlemen, with your permission a piece will be performed tomorrow called *The Insolence of the Pit Chastised* in as many acts as may be desired, by the Marquis de Tenteniac." Such was his renown and prowess that not one member of the audience took up his challenge.

In the ritual of the duel, the insult was followed by the sending of a cartel. This written missive expressed the nature of the insult and the desire for satisfaction. The tone of the cartel was important in determining if the aggrieved parties might be reconciled or not. One handbook advises that 'the most accredited mode is to conduct the whole affair with the greatest possible politeness, expressing the challenge clearly, avoiding strong language, simply stating, first, the cause of offence; secondly, the reason why it is considered a duty to notice the matter, thirdly, naming a friend; and lastly, requesting the appointing of a time and place'. And, as an addendum – '...if abroad, it is proper to state at the foot of the letter the length of the challenger's sword-blade; and a correct copy should be kept of all correspondence that takes place.' Thus, something like '*Signore, s'il suo coraggio è grande come la sua impudenza, m'incontra questa sera nel bosco*' (Sir, if your courage is equal to your impudence, you will meet me tonight in the wood) was considered exemplary. However this, from a young man to a barrister whom he claimed had unfairly cross-examined him, was probably over-stated:

> *Sir; You are renowned for great activity with your tongue, and justly, as circumstances that have occurred today render evident. I am celebrated for my activity with another weapon, equally annoying and destructive; and if you would oblige me by appointing a time and place, it would afford me the greatest gratification to give you a specimen of my proficiency. Your most obedient...*

In the USA, where no specifically American code of honour existed, the cartel became much more of a public statement, and was known as 'posting'. The practice was said to have been instigated by General James Wilkinson. In 1807 he challenged Congressman John Randolph, who declined the offer on the grounds that he was not prepared to descend to the general's level. This did little to placate Wilkinson. He replied:

THE DECADENT SPORTSMAN

You cannot descend to my level! – vain, equivocal thing! And you believe this dastardly subterfuge will avail you, or that your lion's skin will longer conceal your true character? Embrace the alternative, still in your reach, and ascend to the level of a gentleman, if possible, act like a man, if you can, and spare me the pain of publishing you to the world for an insolent, slanderous, prevaricating poltroon.

In the absence of a response, Wilkinson posted the following:

HECTOR UNMASKED: In justice to my character, I denounce to the world John Randolph, a member of Congress, as a prevaricating, base, calumniating scoundrel, poltroon and coward.

After this, posting became commonplace, to the point where sizeable sections of newspapers were taken up with this sort of bluster.

In a contemporary setting, as an epigone of the cartel, one thinks immediately of Mohammed Ali's versifying prior to a bout:

When George Foreman meets me,
He'll pay his debt.
I can drown the drink of water, and kill a dead tree.
Wait till you see Muhammad Ali.

It falls some way short of Oscar Wilde. And it provides clear evidence for the contention that sportsmen today are semi-literate, ill-educated and lacking any of the literary refinement of their forebears.

At the same time as the cartel is sent, seconds are appointed. These will make the necessary negotiations and arrangements for the duel, settling on a time and place. They will, in certain circumstances, try to reach an amicable solution to the dispute. They should be men of maturity, moral courage and worldliness, qualities no self-respecting Decadent would ever possess or admit to. 'There is not one cause in fifty where discreet seconds might not settle the difference and reconcile the parties before they came into the field,' wrote Bosquett. Others contended that 'it is not the sword or the pistol that kills, but the seconds'. In making a choice, there are two groups that should be avoided: Infidels (because, according to Brantôme, 'it is not proper that an unbeliever should witness the shedding of Christian blood, which would delight him.') and Irishmen (because 'nine out of ten Irishmen have such an innate love of fighting that they cannot bring an affair to an amicable adjustment.') This was borne out by an account of a 19th century duel in Dublin where an English doctor commented:

Whilst charging the pistols, our opponent's second addressed himself to my friend in these words: "Sir I am glad to meet you here; I have an affair to settle with you the moment this is over, if you survive my friend."

An important duty of the seconds was to prepare the weapons. This provided occasion for incompetence – as when a pistol was cocked on such a hair trigger that it went off while being held at a duellist's side and blew his foot off – or skullduggery, such as rifling the barrel. Duelling pistols were notoriously inaccurate, but rifling, whether at the muzzle end or the ball end, reduced the inaccuracy and was therefore considered ungentlemanly.

No Decadent duellist, of course, should ever be so imaginatively blinkered as to settle for pistols or swords as the weapon of choice. This displays a distinct lack of aesthetic sensibility. Take a lead from Cagliostro, arch charlatan, alchemist and forger, who was called out by a physician whom he had described as a quack. Arguing that a medical dispute should be settled medically, Cagliostro suggested that each duellist choose one of two pills to swallow; one poisonous, the other harmless. More brutal and exquisite was the choice of weapons agreed upon by Lenfant and Mellant, two gentlemen who, one evening in September 1843, fell out over a game of billiards. The black ball was the weapon and lots were drawn as to who should make the first attempt. Mellant threw first. The ball struck Lenfant's forehead with such force that it killed him outright.

In addition to an odd choice of weapon, the Decadent duellist should consider a less than ordinary venue, certainly not some muddy field at a ludicrously early time of day. When Sainte-Beuve arrived at just such a duelling ground to fight a newspaper editor – duels between writers are not only commonplace, but particularly vicious – he held his pistol in his right hand and an umbrella in his left, saying that he didn't mind being shot, but he was damn'd if he was going to catch a cold. At the other extreme, in 1806 Humphrey Howarth, MP for Evesham, removed all his clothing prior to his duel with Lord Barrymore. His lordship was somewhat taken aback and finding the idea of shooting a naked man preposterous, he went home. The reason Howarth had presented himself in his birthday suit was that as a former Indian Army surgeon, he knew that bullet wounds were far more difficult to deal with when the hole was stuffed with shreds of clothing. What is not known is the pose that Howarth would have struck in this duel. The received wisdom was to turn sideways to one's opponent so as to present as narrow a target as possible. Charles James Fox never bothered with this nicety. 'I am as thick one way as the other,' he remarked. Howarth might have done well to 'tuck himself in', so to speak, or even turn his buttocks towards Barrymore.

An amusing alternative to a natural setting is what Osip Mandelstam refers to as '...the cuckoo duel – that duel in which the opponents stood in a dark room and fired their pistols into cabinets of chinaware, into ink pots, and family portraits...' An American version of the cuckoo duel bore all the hallmarks of that nation's capacity to vulgarise any noble practice. After one of the Yankee antagonists had fired into the darkness and missed his target, the other began stumbling around the room, intent on finishing off his enemy. After much fruitless groping he realised that the only hiding place left in the room was the chimney. He promptly shoved his pistol up the dark orifice and threatened to shoot unless the other paid the debt he owed. The fugitive whimpered his agreement and descended from his sooty chamber, but not before his assailant had taken a knife and cut a square of cloth out of the seat of the fugitive's breeches as a bond.

If the darkened room with inaccurate weapons reduced the duel to a farce, the *duel au mouchoir* really was a deadly affair. The duel got its name from the fact that each duellist held onto a corner of the same handkerchief as they fought. Such an arrangement was a mark of truly intense hatred between two rivals. Rarely did either survive, although in the case of one celebrated *duel au mouchoir* during the reign of Louis XVIII, only one of the pistols was primed. So the outcome rested entirely on the luck of the draw. An elegant variant on this was a duel fought in Kingston, Jamaica between a French Creole, Henri d'Egeville and a Scottish captain by the name of Stewart. The cause was trivial as usual, but when d'Egeville, the offender, turned up, Stewart suggested that they fight standing in a freshly dug grave deep enough to receive both bodies. The Creole accepted and the handkerchief was gripped by both. As the order to fire was given, the Creole fainted. Stewart left him lying at the bottom of the grave, describing him as a miserable coward and an object too pitiable to excite his anger.

A similar incident – the duel in a confined space – took place between Colonel Barbier-Dufai of the Napoleonic Imperial army and a huge young officer of the Royal Guard. The duelling ground was actually a hackney carriage and the two men were tied together with rope leaving only their right arms free to wield a dagger. At a given signal the carriage set off on two circuits of the Place du Carrousel. When the carriage came to a halt and the seconds opened the door, 'the silence of death was within, amid a sea of blood.' The young guards officer was dead and the colonel seriously wounded. However, he felt that he had given his opponent a fair chance. 'His athletic constitution gave him a great advantage over me, but his hour had come,' he concluded.

A more uplifting tale concerns two Frenchmen, M. de Grandpré and M. de Pique, both of whom were prepared to lay down their lives for one Mlle Tirevit. She was a woman truly worthy of such ardent devotion, having given herself in a generous-hearted manner to both gentlemen, and possibly to many others besides if one were to believe slanderous tongues. Although her name might loosely and unfortunately be translated as 'Miss Pull-Cock', she was a dancer of international repute, and de Grandpré and de Pique decided that such a prize required a duel of lofty and noble ambition. Consequently, at 9 in the morning on May 3, 1808, watched by a large crowd near the Tuileries, they and their seconds climbed into balloons at some 80 feet from each other and rose gracefully into the Parisian sky. At a suitably fatal height they fired off blunderbusses at each other's craft. De Pique's balloon let out a sigh, the basket tilted and he and his second tumbled hundreds of feet to their deaths. De Grandpré, meanwhile, drifted safely to earth some 20 miles from the scene of his triumph.

Medlar and I have contributed our own footnote to the history of duelling. Ours was fought in the Decadent Restaurant. I had overheard him informing the guests on one particular table in a sniggering tone that I had mistaken a Brillat-Savarin recipe for one by Marc-Antoine d'Izard. I could not let such a foul calumny go unanswered. 'At least I can tell the difference between *magret de canard* and veal', I retorted. Medlar looked stunned, as if he had received a slap in the face. I knew I had overstepped the mark, but I was sorely provoked. Medlar demanded immediate satisfaction. I had choice of weapons. I decided on water pistols filled with mulberry vodka, from 6 paces. He agreed, a sardonic smile playing about his lips, as if he was already savouring his revenge. We appointed seconds from among the diners who tried desperately to dissuade us from this foolish course of action. We brushed them aside. On the command Medlar got his shot off first. His discharge missed my face but spattered my left shoulder. Mine, on the other hand, was deadly. It hit him full in the mouth. He staggered backwards, coughing up crimson liquid, and collapsed into the table of diners behind him, sending plates, glasses and food crashing to the floor. Ah,

I thought, if only Papa had been there to witness my triumph!

I turned away, looking for a glass of Krupnik to settle my nerves. Diners gathered anxiously around Medlar, who was still prostrate on the table. An eminent Edinburgh surgeon was tending to him. I heard the phrase 'A&E' and in my confused state thought the Television Network had arrived to film the event. Outwardly calm, I sat at the bar and watched as the surgeon applied a plaster to his neck. Lady Athol stole up and spoke discreetly to me.

'Listen Durian, darling. If you need to disappear for a while you can always use my villa on Lake Maggiore.'

I laughed. 'Disappearing is a Lucan family trait. The Grays always stand their ground.'

A pale young man next to me with a handkerchief pressed to his nose was fighting back the tears. 'How can you sit there laughing when that dear, sweet, beautiful man is lying close to death?' One of the waiters hurried over and said, 'He's asking for you.' I crossed the dining room nonchalantly.

'What is it, Medlar?' I enquired in a bored tone of voice.

'You must get...' he was struggling for breath.

'Get what? Spit it out, man!' I knelt beside him amid the shattered crockery.

'That silk shirt... off your back,' he whispered. I leant in closer.

'Into the wash. Mulberry stains...' he gasped, 'won't... come out.'

The effort was too much for him, and he passed out.

Within a few days, apart from a slight difficulty in swallowing, an unnatural pallor, and his temporary confinement to a wheelchair for dramatic effect, Medlar was as fit as a fiddle. We made a great fuss of him, bathed him in oysters and warm sea-water, dosed him with armagnac and pouchong tea.

As soon as we were alone, he asked, 'Is the shirt recovered?' I assured him that it was. 'Thank God,' he replied. His wise words and my prompt action had preserved its delicate colouring – a softly complex interplay of lilac, lemon and rose. We said no more about the duel, but it was clear from a thousand tiny signals that our friendship was all the deeper.

From a Decadent's perspective, the most interesting duels – apart from those that one fights oneself – are those which overturn the established order of things; the occasions, for example, when rather than being the *cause* of a duel, a woman might be the perpetrator. One of the finest instances of this took place in 1892 between Princess Pauline Metternich, honorary President of the Vienna Musical and Theatrical Exhibition, and Countess Kilmansegg, the President of the Ladies' Committee of the Exhibition. The princess was 'ravishing, elegant and witty', and only lightly touched by scandal. The countess bore a name that had been noted for centuries. Not only was this a duel between two women of very high rank, but the cause of it had nothing do with anything as vulgar as love or jealousy. Rather it was provoked by a disagreement over the preparations and arrangements for a Musical Exhibition. The two women retired to Vaduz, the capital of Lichtenstein, where the duel was fought out with rapiers. The princess suffered a small cut to her nose and the countess was wounded on the arm. Both were ably attended to by the Baroness Lubinska, who held a medical degree.

Such paragons of proto-feminism were nothing in comparison to Julie d'Aubigny, upon whom Théophile Gautier's 1835 novel *Mademoiselle de Maupin,* is based. La

Maupin, married at an early age, eloped soon after with a lover who had taught her to fence with very great skill. They headed south, giving exhibitions of swordplay to make money, and ended up singing in the theatre in Marseilles. At about this time La Maupin fell in love with a young woman whose parents, noticing the infatuation, packed her off to a nunnery in Avignon to protect her from La Maupin's malign influence. Not to be deterred, La Maupin presented herself as a novice to gain entry to the convent and according to Fétis, 'A few days later, a nun died. The actress carried the corpse to her friend's bed, set fire to the bedchamber and in the ensuing tumult, stole away with the object of her affections.' After three months of sapphic ecstasy, the nun returned sheepishly to Avignon and La Maupin headed for Paris where she became a huge favourite at the Opera, in such roles as Dido and, in 1690, as Pallas Athena in *Cadmus et Hermione* by Lully.

Being born with *'des inclinations masculines'* as Fétis puts it, Mlle Maupin often dressed as a man, and acted as one too. To avenge herself for an insult at the hands of one Duménil, a fellow-performer at the Opera, she waited for him in the Place des Victoires and demanded satisfaction. On his refusal to fight she promptly relieved him of his watch and snuffbox. When Duménil was bragging to his friends that he had fought off three ruffians who had carried off his watch and snuffbox, Maupin handed over the items informing all present that she alone had given him a good beating.

Her skill as a swordswoman is best illustrated by a duel she fought during the course of a ball given by Monsieur, Louis XIV's brother. Her opponents were the three suitors of a young woman to whom La Maupin had addressed indecent suggestions before kissing her full on the mouth in the middle of the dance floor. She stepped outside, killed all three and then returned to the ball, told Monsieur of the event and begged his pardon for interrupting his ball.

An even more anomalous duellist, who came a little later than La Maupin, was the enigmatic Chevalier d'Eon – or is that 'Chevalière'? His skill as a swordsman was matched only by the uncertainty that surrounded his gender. The Chevalier found himself in England in the 1770s acting as a diplomat, spy or possibly a double agent for the French, and for a number of complicated reasons was negotiating his return to France. One of the stipulations of the agreement drawn up (known as La Transaction) was that henceforth d'Eon would be required to dress as a woman, or rather 're-dress' as a woman. There is a suggestion that he was indeed born a woman. Rumours of such had followed him around the coffee houses of London and the Chevalier would challenge anyone who voiced any suspicions to back them up with a sword. In France, however, duelling in a crinoline was something of handicap to him. He wrote a letter to the Minister Maurepas, asking him to revoke the order concerning his attire in order to give satisfaction to the son of the Comte de Guerchy, one of d'Eon's bitterest enemies. He wrote: 'I have been able, in obedience to the orders of the late King and his ministers, to remain in petticoats during peacetime; but that is quite out of the question in time of war... I have always acted like Achilles; I never wage war with the dead and I only kill the living.'

It has to be said that D'Eon's female persona drew few admirers. It took four hours to make him presentable for Louis XVI and Marie Antoinette at Versailles in November 1777. Even then the Vicomtesse de Fars noted: 'She had nothing of our sex but the petticoats and the curls, which suited her horribly.' And walking in high heels was a social skill that d'Eon never mastered.

The decline of duelling followed inevitably upon the decline of the aristocracy and the ethos of the gentleman with its attendant obsession with honour. Of course there has been much discussion and disputation over how a gentleman is to be defined or recognised. One of the clearest definitions states that a gentleman is one who would do things that no gentleman would ever think of doing in a manner only a gentleman knows how. However, once duels of 'honour' were being fought between a part-time linen-draper from Tottenham Court Road and an inn-keeper's nephew from Taunton as in 1838, it was clear the game was no longer worth the candle.

The key to the duel had always been its ritualistic element, the stylishness with which one faced the possibility of death and the carelessness of personal safety in pursuit of a higher ideal. Once that went, there was little point to the duel. Nowhere was this more evident than in America, where any sense of ritual seems to have been lost on the general populace. This is Bronson Howard writing about the myth and reality of the American duel:

The Italian firmly believes – which belief, by the way, he also shares with the Frenchman – that when two Americans wish to fight a duel, they load one pistol, draw lots for it, and the winner shoots himself. Why this should be supposed to be the American way of duelling I cannot imagine. If there is any such thing as an "American" duel, it is what is familiarly known as "shooting on sight". The challenger sends word to his enemy that he will shoot him the next time he sees him, and thereupon the latter arms himself, and takes his walks abroad with much caution, until the two meet, when both begin a brisk fusillade with their revolvers, and one of them is usually killed, together with from four to six of the bystanders. This sort of duel would never do for a sparsely-populated country like Italy; and as for the other and falsely called "American duel", it lacks everything that could recommend it to the lover of athletic sports.

The history of duelling is rich in descriptions of bizarre characters, encounters and outcomes. Much rarer are accounts told from the interior, so to speak. To describe what it is like to be inside the head of one who is about to fight a duel takes a peculiar genius. Guy de Maupassant, inveterate adulterer and epic philanderer, had more experience than most of the inner emotions of the duellist. He no doubt drew upon this for his short story, *A Coward*. It is a jewelled masterpiece, like one of the scintillating brooches worn by the great New Orleans mulatto duellist, Basile Croquère. At this point in the story, the Vicomte Gontran-Joseph de Signoles, or "Beau Signoles" as he was known in society, has issued a challenge and is in his lodgings the night before he is due to fight his first duel.

And he suddenly determined to get up and look at himself in the glass. He lighted his candle. When he saw his face reflected in the mirror it was barely recognisable. He seemed to see before him a stranger. His eyes looked disproportionately large, and he was deathly pale.

He remained standing in front of the mirror. He stuck out his tongue, as if to examine the state of his health, and all at once a thought flashed into his mind:

"By this time the day after tomorrow I might well be dead."

And his heart throbbed painfully.

"At this time the day after tomorrow I may be dead.

This person in front of me, this 'I' whom I see in the glass, will perhaps be no more. What! Here I am, I look at myself, I feel myself to be alive – and yet in twenty-four hours I may be lying on that bed, with closed eyes, dead, cold, inanimate."

He turned round, and could see himself distinctly lying on his back on the couch he had just quitted. He had the hollow face and the limp hands of death.

Then he became afraid of his bed, and to avoid seeing it went to his smoking-room. He mechanically took a cigar, lighted it, and began walking back and forth. He was cold; he took a step toward the bell, to wake his valet, but stopped with hand raised toward the bell rope.

"He would see that I am afraid!"

And, instead of ringing, he made a fire himself. His hands quivered nervously as they touched various objects. His head grew dizzy, his thoughts confused, disjointed, painful; a numbness seized his spirit, as if he had been drinking.

And all the time he kept on saying:

"What shall I do? What will become of me?"

His whole body trembled spasmodically; he rose, and, going to the window, drew back the curtains.

The day – a summer day – was breaking. The pink sky cast a glow on the city, its roofs, and its walls. A flush of light enveloped the awakened world, like a caress from the rising sun, and the glimmer of dawn kindled new hope in the breast of the vicomte. What a fool he was to let himself succumb to fear before anything was decided – before his seconds had interviewed those of Georges Lamil, before he even knew whether he would have to fight or not!

He bathed, dressed, and left the house with a firm step.

He repeated as he went:

"I must be firm – very firm. I must show that I am not afraid."

His seconds, the marquis and the colonel, placed themselves at his disposal, and, having shaken him warmly by the hand, began to discuss details.

"You want a serious duel?" asked the colonel.

"Yes – quite serious," replied the vicomte.

"You insist on pistols?" put in the marquis.

"Yes."

"Do you leave all the other arrangements in our hands?"

With a dry, jerky voice the vicomte answered:

"Twenty paces – at a given signal – the arm to be raised, not lowered – shots to be exchanged until one or other is seriously wounded."

"Excellent conditions," declared the colonel in a satisfied tone. "You are a good shot; all the chances are in your favour."

And they parted. The vicomte returned home to wait for them. His agitation, only temporarily allayed, now increased momentarily. He felt, in arms, legs and chest, a sort of trembling – a continuous vibration; he could not stay still, either sitting or standing. His mouth was parched, and he made every now and then a clicking movement of the tongue, as if to detach it from his palate.

He attempted to take luncheon, but could not eat. Then it occurred to him to seek courage in drink, and he sent for a decanter of rum, of which he swallowed, one after another, six small glasses.

A burning warmth, followed by a deadening of the mental faculties, ensued. He said to himself:

"I know how to manage. Now it will be all right!"

But at the end of an hour he had emptied the decanter, and his agitation was worse than ever. A mad longing possessed him to throw himself on the ground, to bite, to scream. Night fell.

A ring at the bell so unnerved him that he had not the strength to rise to receive his seconds.

He dared not even to speak to them, wish them good-day, utter a single word, lest his changed voice should betray him.

"All is arranged as you wished," said the colonel. "Your adversary claimed at first the privilege of the offended part; but he yielded almost at once, and accepted your conditions. His seconds are two military men."

"Thank you," said the vicomte.

The marquis added:

"Please excuse us if we do not stay now, for we have a good deal to see to yet. We shall want a reliable doctor, since the duel is not to end until a serious wound has been inflicted; and you know that bullets are not to be trifled with. We must select a spot near some house to which the wounded party can be carried if necessary. In fact, the arrangements will take us another two or three hours at least."

The vicomte articulated for the second time:

"Thank you."

"You're all right?" asked the colonel. "Quite calm?"

"Perfectly calm, thank you."

THE DECADENT SPORTSMAN

The two men withdrew.

When he was once more alone he felt as though he should go mad. His servant having lighted the lamps, he sat down at his table to write some letters. When he had traced at the top of a sheet of paper the words: "This is my last will and testament," he started from his seat, feeling himself incapable of connected thought, of decision in regard to anything.

So he was going to fight! He could no longer avoid it. What, then, possessed him? He wished to fight, he was fully determined to fight, and yet, in spite of all his mental effort, in spite of the exertion of all his will power, he felt that he could not even preserve the strength necessary to carry him through the ordeal. He tried to conjure up a picture of the duel, his own attitude, and that of his enemy.

Every now and then his teeth chattered audibly. He thought he would read, and took down Chateauvillard's Rules of Duelling. *Then he said:*

"Is the other man practised in the use of the pistol? Is he well known? How can I find out?"

He remembered Baron de Vaux's book on marksmen, and searched it from end to end. Georges Lamil was not mentioned. And yet, if he were not an adept, would he have accepted without demur such a dangerous weapon and such deadly conditions?

He opened a case of Gastinne Renettes which stood on a small table, and took from it a pistol. Next he stood in the correct attitude for firing, and raised his arm. But he was trembling from head to foot, and the weapon shook in his grasp.

Then he said to himself:

"It is impossible. I cannot fight like this."

He looked at the little black, death-spitting hole at the end of the pistol; he thought of dishonour, of the whispers at the clubs, the smiles in his friends' drawing-rooms, the contempt of women, the veiled sneers of the newspapers, the insults that would be hurled at him by cowards.

He still looked at the weapon, and raising the hammer, saw the glitter of the priming below it. The pistol had been left loaded by some chance, some oversight. And the discovery rejoiced him, he knew not why.

If he did not maintain, in presence of his opponent, the steadfast bearing which was so necessary to his honour, he would be ruined forever. He would be branded, stigmatised as a coward, hounded out of society! And he felt, he knew, that he could not maintain that calm, unmoved demeanour. And yet he was brave, since the thought that followed was not even rounded to a finish in his mind; but, opening his mouth wide, he suddenly plunged the barrel of the pistol as far back as his throat, and pressed the trigger.

When the valet, alarmed at the report, rushed into the room he found his master lying dead upon his back. A spurt of blood had splashed the white paper on the table, and had made a great crimson stain beneath the words:

"This is my last will and testament."

4

THE RIDER

'I can tell everything I want to know about a man from the way he sits on a horse.'
                                   (Hugh Lowther, 5th Earl of Lonsdale)

Leopardstown Race Course, Co. Dublin
Dark vortices of memory began to spin in my hippocampus as I watched Brazilian Shave cross the finishing line in the Irish Champions' Hurdle. He had won by a length at 100 to 1, with a farmer's boy on his back. An impossible victory. Questions were being asked. Down at the rail, one or two tweed caps were flying, but for the most part it was long, sullen faces.
'What the hell happened there?'
'I never liked the look of that race.'
'That's a bloody steal.'
'It's a great day for the bookies.'
'When is it not?'
I had seen the odds on High Wind, the favourite, flickering in blood-red points of light on the bookmakers' boards. I had slapped a hasty tenner on the outsider. When the gleaming bronze neck of Brazilian Shave surged out of the ruck at the last fence, leaving the others in a flailing knot of anonymity, I was seized by a race-goer's schizophrenic frenzy of excitement and fear – would he win? Would he fall? Would he fade? In the wildfire of that final furlong I was suddenly reminded of the distant afternoon when my aunt Venetia had brought me to this

spot, aged nine, to blood me in the Sport of Kings.

'Many of the family have been ruined by horses, Medlar,' she said. 'It's a proud Lucan tradition.'

This made no sense to my innocent mind. 'How can you be ruined by a horse?' I asked.

'Let me show you.' She unclasped her vast crocodile-skin handbag, its halves splayed like the jaws of a sinister black mouth. 'Here's £1000 in cash. You're going to place a bet.'

She pointed a jewelled index finger at the row of bookmakers, who stood like targets in a shooting gallery, each under a little blackboard chalked with names and numbers.

'Choose one of those fellows over there.'

They were a collection of humanity's odder types. A barrel-stomached man with a shiny bowler hat, sagging cheeks, and ginger whiskers that flapped like loose trousers in the wind. To his left, a living skeleton in a spotted bow tie and check shooting jacket. To his right, a grinning ventriloquist's dummy with badly dyed orange hair, brown suit, yellow shirt, and thin mauve tie. His skin was white and waxy, his eyes melancholy and in separate orbits: one surveying the crowd, the other corkscrewing neurotically down to the wad of banknotes in his hand. A sign above his head read *Lucky Jim Fenimore, the Punter's Friend.*

'That one,' I said.

'Now choose a horse from the card.'

I studied the names: Purple Haze, Fred Astaire, Big Fairy, Camp Fire, Bolshevik King, Fancy Dan, Humidor, Folding Chair...

'Camp Fire,' I said.

She seemed displeased. 'That's 66 to 1.'

'So?'

'He hasn't got a hope in hell.'
'Why is he running?'
'You may well ask.'
'How much will we get if he wins?'
'£66,000.'
'And if he loses?'
'Nothing.'
'What about Fancy Dan?'
'He's the favourite at 7 to 4. You'll only get 1750 on your 1000.'
'I prefer Camp Fire.'
'Then place the bet.'
'But if he hasn't got a hope...'
'If you have the hunch, do the deed!'

I approached Lucky Jim, who engaged me suspiciously with his downward-swivelling eye. 'I'd like to make a bet of a thousand pounds on Camp Fire,' I said.

'Win or place?'
'Win.'

He looked appalled. 'Are you sure?'
'Quite sure.'
'How old are you?'

I glimpsed a sign: MINIMUM AGE 18 YEARS.
'19,' I said.

He glanced around with his spare eye. 'You're very young for 19,' he growled.

'It's a rare medical condition.'
'Too rare for me, lad. Come and see me when you're 29.'

Aunt Venetia saw my struggle. 'He's with me, Mr Fenimore!'

'Look here, Madam, this is a great deal of money.'
'Do you want the bet or not?'

Lucky Jim was not entirely sure he did. He had a word with the man in the shiny bowler, who glared down at me, my aunt and the odds. He stood paralysed for a moment, divided between greed and fear. Greed won. He nodded brusquely.

'We're on,' said Jim, handing me a slip of paper. His fingers folded like claws around the money.

Aunt Venetia was an unusual woman. With a body like a stubby little powder-keg, she gave no hint of the beauty she had possessed as a girl, when a series of statesmen and tycoons had imperilled their empires by falling under her spell. A photograph in a family album immortalised her moment of perfection in spangled granules of silver as she plunged off a diving-board in Rio de Janeiro, the pale crucifix of her body etched against the dark mass of Corcovado and a thundery summer sky. She was by then the lover of Baldassaro Baldassari, a cattle-rancher and refrigerated-ship magnate from Buenos Aires, who offered her $45 million to become his wife for 12 months – an offer that was regarded at the time, and for many years after, as 'the most expensive shag in history'. She had already scorched an impressive path through the bedrooms of Paris and London – from the humblest of beginnings. A transvestite stable lad at 16, she had gone on to ride for the Earl of Lonsdale in the 1920s, winning a number of classic races for his stable. The grandees of the turf courted her – Lord Essenham, Pierre d'Este, the Maharajah of Pujamuna – men who relied heavily on the aphrodisiac powers of a well-stuffed wallet and a hand-made silk hat. She mentioned their names with no sign of special regard, with boredom even – they were as foothills to the mighty peak of Lonsdale.

'Lordy', as she called him, had been her first hero. He should also be mine, she believed. 'He was glamorous to his fingertips,' she murmured, with a distant light in her eyes. Had they been lovers? One felt sure of it. Gay or straight? That was trickier. She had been his stable boy... Gay perhaps to start with, but straightening as the jodhpurs and silks fell away. That must have caused some wild surmise in the hayloft: the surprising softness and fullness of the pectoral muscles, the absence turning to dark presence in the crotch. I enjoyed the thought of it. The ambiguity set fires smouldering in my mind.

How shrewd she was in her choice of mentor! One could not ask for a more decadent sportsman than The Yellow Earl.

He was born with few prospects. The family owned coal and iron mines, castles, farms, forests, the town of Whitehaven, a symphony orchestra, a house in Newmarket, a shooting estate in Rutland, Lakes Windermere and Hawes Water, a pair of steam yachts, and two enormous London mansions, but Hugh was merely the second son and knew from an early age that he had no hope of a title or a fortune. What lesser spirits would have regarded as a disadvantage he turned into a licence for freedom, running wild on the family's estates, enjoying the fullest possible physical life among the grooms and farmhands, while abhorring the classroom and all forms of constraint. His father, the Earl of Lonsdale, a keen fox-hunting man, thoroughly approved. His mother, Pussy Lonsdale, did not. She persuaded her husband to send Hugh to Eton. It made no impression. Nor did a private tutor. He was trundled off to a finishing school in Switzerland, which he failed to finish. He joined a travelling circus. His 18th birthday, celebrated in a caravan in the Low Countries, triggered a faint memory, he was not sure what, but an instinct made him return to Lowther Castle in time to collect the first instalment of an allowance of £1,000 a year.

When the 3rd Earl died, Hugh's elder brother St George

inherited the title and estates. St George was a shy, bookish recluse, ill at ease in the role of grandee. Hugh felt he could do the job much better. To set an example, he lived vastly beyond his means, courting scandal in the company of prize fighters, jockeys, dandies, sportsmen and actresses. His brother seemed to take the hint, and died of influenza only six years after inheriting. Hugh, at the age of 25, became one of the richest men in England.

He slipped effortlessly into the part. With a fresh gardenia in his button-hole each day, he set about the monumental task of spending every penny of his £200,000 annual allowance. He had a certain amount of help: 100 servants and administrators, including a Chamberlain, a Master of Horse, a Groom of the Bedchamber, and a Master of Music. The servants wore bright yellow jackets with blue facings and white buckskin breeches. (One of them observed that 'he would have painted *us* yellow if he could'.) The household moved between London and the country in a privately chartered train. If the journey involved a night on board, he took a first-class sleeper for himself and another for his dogs.

He began collecting horses, and laid down strict guidelines as to their size: chestnuts had to be no more than 15 hands 2 inches in height and 1008 lb in weight; hunters no less than 16 hands high and 6 feet in girth. The numbers are insignificant, of course. It is the insistence on them that marks him out as a Decadent. His wife, Grace, had a horse collection of her own, and rode daily in Hyde Park, noted always for her elegance and the 'symmetry, action and good manners' of her mount.

Lonsdale was also a keen motorist, and a founder member of the Automobile Association, whose yellow livery was copied from his own. (Today's 'AA', a commercial organisation largely devoted to the sale of insurance and the dissemination of lower middle-class values, bears no relation to its great progenitor.)

Fox-hunting was an ancestral obsession of the Lowthers, and the Quorn under Hugh's Mastership became legendary for its extravagant standards of smartness. Crowds gathered to watch them set out, with their white leather breeches and dark red coats, their thoroughbred chestnut horses and immaculate pedigree hounds. Very little of the cost was covered by subscriptions; most came from Hugh's pocket. The managers of the Lonsdale estate despaired. They seemed to spend their lives on the edge of bankruptcy.

Beside horse-racing and hunting Hugh's greatest love was boxing. He worked hard to legalise the sport, bringing it out of the illicit clubs that he had frequented in his youth. He created the Lonsdale Belt for British champions, a curiously gladiatorial garment consisting of a broad band of red, white and blue striped fabric, overlaid with gold strapwork and medallions, all gathering to a baroque jeweller's climax in a hideous central buckle framing a portrait of the great man in porcelain.

Boxer, huntsman, sailor, racing fanatic, Hugh dedicated his life and fortune to sport. He was disliked and envied by his peers, but adored by the working class. When he appeared at Ascot in his bright yellow carriage with liveried postillions, he was greeted by loud cheers from the crowd. They preferred him, strangely enough, to the bearded chap in the drab vehicle in front, the one with royal arms painted on the door.

Venetia's service to the Yellow Earl set her up for life. Her years at the front end of racing were lived hard. She had subjected herself to the champion jockey's weight-loss regime, known as 'wasting' – a daily eight-mile run wearing three sets of long johns, a rubber suit and five woollen jumpers, then an hour in a Turkish bath and a massage in sweat; nothing for dinner but steak and champagne. She had ridden and fallen many times. She was fit, tough, fearless and disciplined. With money in the bank and a yearning for adventure, she sailed first to Le Havre, then – after nine months of sexual havoc in Paris and Deauville – to Rio, for her destined meeting with Baldassaro Baldassari.

The beef baron turned out to be considerably more amusing than she had bargained for, and the $45-million dollar shag evolved into a long and unfashionably happy marriage. She lost interest in sex several years before he did, and encouraged him to take his opportunities wherever he found them. When the old boy died, aged 80, during a post-coital siesta with one of the chambermaids on his yacht *Messalina*, Venetia was left with three sons, an immeasurable fortune, and a determination to continue adventuring long into the twilight. She returned to racing as an owner and bloodstock breeder. Every summer she organised a point-to-point at Pharsalia, the Lucan seat in Bedfordshire. She did charitable work in exotic places, gave money to retirement homes for injured horses, shattered jockeys and ruined owners, and began work on a monumental history of racing, which she proposed to call *Kings of the Turf*. Meanwhile her children developed in interesting ways. One son took over the beef farms, another the refrigerated ships, the third became a pornographic film producer and magazine publisher.

Kings of the Turf was never finished, but it gave her life a purpose. She worked in the library at Pharsalia for weeks at a time. She left me the manuscript in her will, twelve boxes of the stuff, in the hope that I might complete it one day – a monstrous and unlikely prospect, particularly as there were no funds attached to pay for the work. Much of it is unreadable – rambling, ranting, sentimental – but by no means is it all bad. The section on Newmarket gives a flavour of her writing:

In 1603 King James I, on his journey from Edinburgh to London, was forced by heavy fog to stay overnight in the village of Newmarket. The next day – the fog having lifted, or he wouldn't have seen a damn thing – he noted the springy turf and open landscape of Newmarket Heath, and thought fondly of his horses in Edinburgh. How they would have loved running here! How firm the footing! How soft the air! At once he sent for them. There were no horse boxes in those days, so he... well, what the hell did he do? Put them on a bloody great waggon? Horse-drawn no doubt! Maybe walked them down?? Two hundred and fifty miles!! Bonkers. Or brought them by ship. Makes more sense. Anyway, he set up a racing stable, and around that he established a whole summer court, so anyone who wanted to see him about matters of state had to come up to Newmarket and talk around the races, and he'd be saying, "That's all very well, Mr Bacon, the Exchequer must be balanced, but what dost thou fancie in the 2.30?" First principle of the nation's life: business of state, no matter how high or pressing, must never be allowed to interfere with sport. Sir Francis Drake showed the same doughty spirit fifty years before in Plymouth. "We'll finish our game of bowls, go down to ye pub for a pint, have a few pies, and then – only then – we shall see about sending those damned lisping conquistadores to the bottom of the ocean." Or words to that effect.

Strange echo of this 350 years later: another

invasion crisis, another hour of need, and there's my friend Douglas Bader calmly making arrangements for a squash match from the radio in his Spitfire as he climbed to meet German bombers over the North Sea. Cocky Dundas heard it and wrote: 'The conversation had a decidedly calming effect on my nerves... It was extraordinary enough that a man with two tin legs should have been thinking about squash in any circumstances. That he should be doing so while leading three squadrons of Hurricanes and two of Spitfires into battle against the Luftwaffe was even more extraordinary. Here, quite clearly, was a man made in the mould of Francis Drake – a man to be followed, a man who would win.'

I love all race-courses, and if each has its pros and cons, Newmarket is my favourite, with its velvety turf flowing like emerald silk. The races here are more fun too. Here is the Newmarket Journal *in 1875:*

'After a week at Ascot or Epsom, a visit to Goodwood, or a trip to Liverpool, what are one's experiences? A struggle at railway stations to obtain a seat, a struggle up dusty hills leading to the scene of the sport, almost a hand-to-hand fight to get into or out of the ring, into or out of the saddling paddock, up to the top of the stand or down again; while all the time one's ears are dinned by the never-ceasing Babel of voices from which there is no escape; or the most desperate struggle of all, to get home at the end of the day, remains to be undergone. In fact, at the close of an ordinary race week the visitor finds himself reduced to the last stage of physical exhaustion, but at Newmarket he can enjoy racing without the necessity of exertion and without incurring fatigue.

'He can drive – or better still ride – pretty much where he likes. The Heath is open to him, and he can suit his own tastes. He can gallop down to see the start, or station himself at the Bushes or some favourite point where racing veterans say they can always pick out the winner as the horses flash by, or he can remain near the judge's chair and enjoy the excitement of a well-contested finish. There is no mob of excursionists, with their ginger-beer bottles and sandwich bags; there are no nigger minstrels, no acrobats, no comic singers with their knee-breeches and shillelaghs, and no army of policemen shouting out that the course must be cleared. The few hundred spectators know very well when to get off the course without being told, the numbers go up at the appointed moment with military punctuality, the horses canter past you to the starting-post, each accompanied by his own select following of admirers or critics, the white flag – they always use a white flag at Newmarket – is elevated for a moment and then falls, for the starter's patience is rarely taxed, the horses sweep by, and the race is over without any fuss, disturbance or difficulty.'

This was the atmosphere that we liked to encourage when we held races at Pharsalia. It was one big party, as horses and riders galloped around the estate and the neighbouring countryside in a wild and merry steeplechase: twenty-three fences in total, through the dairy farm, across the golf course, round the lake, and up the avenue of Spanish chestnuts to the finish! The rules were very simple (don't fall off), the betting unofficial, and the event enjoyed by the locals for many years until the beastly gendarmerie closed the whole thing down

> *under a collection of poisonous Acts of Parliament: the Gaming Act, the Golf Courses Protection Act, and the Suppression of Country Pleasures Act.*
>
> *Newmarket, alas, is rapidly going the way of Epsom and the rest under this appalling brainless onslaught of officialdom...*

I suspect that Venetia's liking for Newmarket had another motive, which she chose not to reveal. Newmarket was the favourite haunt of Aly Khan, the only man who, in her racing days, rivalled the Earl of Lonsdale.

Aly was the son and heir apparent of the Aga Khan, and would have succeeded his father as the leader of the Ismaili sect if he had not proved so thoroughly unsuited to great office – or indeed office of any kind. Among the thousand or more girls that he bedded in his princely career, Venetia was certainly one. Quintin Gilbey states that in the 1930s 'it became a status symbol among the international set to have been to bed with Aly.' He describes the man's style: 'A friend once confided to me that he had irrefutable proof that Aly Khan had been to bed with his wife and his girl friend in the same week, and that he was going to kill him. But when I met him a week or so later he told me that Aly had been so charming when he had run into him at Epsom that he couldn't bring himself to refer to the matter, especially after Aly had told him to back one of his horses which had won.'

There was discipline behind the ease. Gilbey reports that Aly 'attributed his success to a course of study under an old Arab doctor in Cairo who, forty years earlier, had given his father similar instruction. The technique is known as *imsac*, which means "retaining", and no man who has mastered it will ever reach his climax till his partner has derived full satisfaction. He told me that by exercising mind over matter, he could prolong sexual enjoyment almost indefinitely. This was confirmed to me by four women, all married, who told me that they had not known the meaning of sex till they experienced it with Aly. Aly concluded the discussion by saying, with a twinkle in his eye: 'I picked up more useful information from that old man in Cairo than you ever did in all the time you were at Eton.'

'Such was his charm,' Gilbey concludes, 'that he made a generous contribution to the happiness of his fellow beings in the forty-nine years of his life... As he had never been subjected to any real discipline, and was the possessor of an indulgent father with a bottomless pocket, it was surprising that he was not a great deal more spoilt than he was.'

It was Venetia's son Beniamino, the film producer, who telephoned me one day from Buenos Aires to ask if I knew anything about 'a pair of English eccentrics who create the most outrageous work under the oddest of pseudonyms'.

'You must be thinking of Medlar Lucan and Durian Gray,' I said.

'No. Just one name each.'

'Gilbert and George?'

'No.'

I began scraping the barrel. 'Morecambe and Wise?'

'No.'

'Randall and Hopkirk (Deceased)?

'No.'

'Godley and Creme?'

'No.'

'How about Derek and Clive?'

'That's it!'

He told me his mother had heard a horse-racing commentary by Derek and Clive, and loved it so much she wanted it performed at a memorial service for Baldassaro. Could I find it?

I said I possibly could, but that Derek and Clive's work was not often heard on solemn occasions.

'Why not?' he asked.

'It reads like an attempt to get into *The Guinness Book of Records*. For smut.'

'That sounds just right for mother.'

I promised to do what I could. Peter Cook and Dudley Moore, the progenitors of Derek & Clive, had both died – a great loss to the British nation, which ought to have been marked by a state funeral and public eruptions of grief at least as volcanic as those unleashed by the death of Princess Diana. But the national priorities are bizarre. And Peter Cook's book of scripts, *Tragically I Was an Only Twin,* had remained as a monument to the great man. In honour of my Aunt Venetia, and the randy Don Baldassaro, I here give the text of Derek and Clive's *Horse Racing*:

DUDLEY: Good afternoon and welcome to racing at Newmarket. They're about to go into the stalls for the three thirty, so over to you, Peter.
PETER: Thank you. Yes, the seven runners for this Durex handicap over six furlongs just begin to load up. That's The Poof, very much on his toes, and beautifully turned out. He really looked a picture in the paddock. Just coming into our picture is Vagina. Vagina's one of the fillies in the race. She's very good speed. The

overnight rain will have helped her. She likes it a bit soft underfoot. That's The Wanker, going into the stalls. A steady performer, The Wanker, but he tends to be a bit one-paced. Just going in is Buttocks. Buttocks, a big colt, blinkered for the first time. And there's our favourite, The Prick. I think he would have preferred slightly firmer going. And just going in is the outsider of the field, the seven-year-old Arsehole. Arsehole by Shit out of Bumhole. He's been tailed off on his last three outings – rather disappointing horse, this. And one of the last to go in is Big Tits, who's carrying the top weight. Steady performer, but I think that ten-pound penalty will be a little too much for her this afternoon. She's safely in. Oh dear, The Prick is rearing up. He tends to get excited – a very excitable horse. I remember he had to be withdrawn at Lingfield. Yes, they're going to put the hood on him. They're very good, the handlers here at Newmarket. And now a late show of betting.

DUDLEY: *Thank you, Peter. The Prick has hardened half a point to eleven to eight, Vagina is threes, The Poof and Buttocks both nine to two, there's been some late money for Big Tits, who's coming to join The Wanker on eight to one, and Arsehole is sixty-six to one.*

PETER: *As expected, Arsehole is the sixty-six to one complete outsider. And they're all in, they're under starter's orders, and they're off! Big Tits got a flyer and is the first to show. Arsehole was slowly away, and as they settle down, it's Big Tits from Vagina with The Prick tucked in behind these two, then comes the blinkered Buttocks, being pressed by The Poof, going steadily behind these five is The Wanker, and trailing the field Arsehole. And as they start to climb the hill, it's Vagina,*

who just shows clear of Buttocks, The Prick is close up third, nothing between these three, Big Tits is to the left, tucked in behind is The Poof, still trailing the field is Arsehole, there is The Poof again, making a challenge, with Arsehole under pressure, but finding nothing. And as they race to the line, it's Vagina being pressed by The Prick, with The Poof making rapid progress, trying to squeeze in between The Buttocks and the rail. The Prick and Vagina, nothing between these two. And The Wanker's coming with a late run, The Wanker is coming with a late run, and Big Tits has dropped out of it altogether. And with a hundred yards to go, it's The Prick and Vagina drawing clear, The Prick and Vagina, it must be a photo, I can't separate them, but I think The Poof takes third from The Wanker and still to finish is the tiring Arsehole. Well, one hell of a race. The Prick may just have got up in the last strides, but I wouldn't like to put my money on it.
DUDLEY: *And now it's back to Topless Darts at Roehampton.*

Back in Leopardstown on that far-off afternoon, I clutched my betting slip tightly and waited for the race to begin. 'They're off,' grunted Aunt Venetia, pointing at a dark smudge on the far side of the valley. At first I saw nothing moving at all. Then the smudge grew bigger, began to ripple and sprout limbs. It expanded as it approached – dark legs doubling and quadrupling, bright arms and caps, a jumble of torsos, angled over eager necks – a flow of dark energy rolling fiercely towards us, seen in momentary hundred-legged profile, then thundering away, round the bend and up the green slope.

About a hundred yards beyond the curve, the pack surged over a jump. A cry went up.

'Johnson's down,' I heard someone say.

A man with binoculars held to his eyes said, 'Fancy Dan's out too. Poor devil can't get up.'

'Shit!' said another.

The black smudge joggled away into the mist.

A second cry, more a kind of groan. 'What the hell was that?'

'Folding Chair... He's folded.'

'And Fred Astaire. No more dancing for him.'

When the pack returned to view, there were just four horses left, the jockeys whipping savagely in the fury of the sprint. One of them seemed suddenly willed forward by a mysterious power. He drew inexorably into the lead, space parting in front of him, while the ones behind laboured more heavily with each step. He crossed the finishing line, the jockey's teeth flashing, whip raised in triumph.

'It's Camp Fire,' said my aunt. 'At sixty-six to one.'

The Punter's Friend had turned grey. Even his orange hair seemed to blaze less brightly.

'I'm not sure I can pay you all at once,' he said.

Poor Lucky Jim. Poor Fancy Dan. Poor Folding Chair and Fred Astaire. They all had bullets in their heads by the end of the day. And I had £66,000 in my pocket – a substantial and intoxicating sum for a nine-year-old.

5

THE GYMNAST

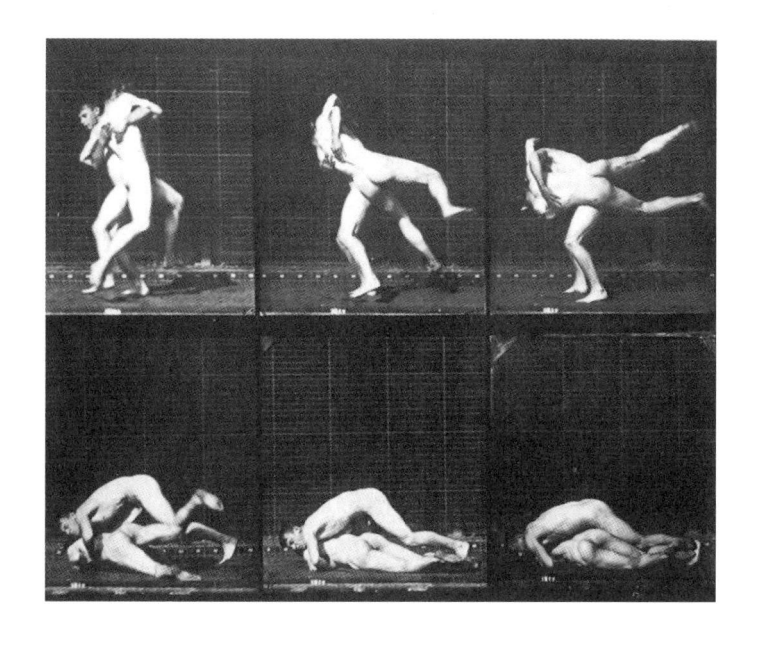

He showed me an enclosed space and an open door over against the wall.

And there, he said, is the building at which we all meet: and a goodly company we are.

And what is this building, I asked; and what sort of entertainment have you?

The building, he replied, is a newly erected Palaistra; and the entertainment is generally conversation, to which you are welcome.

Thank you, I said; and is there any teacher there?

Yes, he said, your old friend and admirer, Miccus.

Indeed, I replied; he is a very eminent professor.

Are you disposed, he said, to go with me and see them?

Yes, I said; but I should like to know first, what is expected of me, and who is the favourite among you?

Some persons have one favourite, Socrates, and some another, he said.

And who is yours? I asked: tell me that, Hippothales.

At this he blushed; and I said to him, O Hippothales, thou son of Hieronymus! do not say that you are, or that you are not, in love; the confession is too late; for I see that you are not only in love, but are already far gone in your love. Simple and foolish as I am, the Gods have given me the power of understanding affections of this kind.

Whereupon he blushed more and more.

Ctesippus said: I like to see you blushing, Hippothales, and hesitating to tell Socrates the name; when, if he were with you but for a very short time, you would have plagued him to death by talking about nothing else. Indeed, Socrates, he has literally deafened us, and stopped our ears with the praises of Lysis; and if he is a little intoxicated, there is every likelihood that we may have our sleep murdered with a cry of Lysis. His performances in prose are bad enough, but nothing at all in comparison with his verse; and when he drenches us with his poems and other compositions, it is really too bad; and worse still is his manner of singing them to his love; he has a voice which is truly appalling, and we cannot help hearing him: and now having a question put to him by you, behold he is blushing.

Who is Lysis? I said: I suppose that he must be young; for the name does not recall any one to me.

Why, he said, his father being a very well known man, he retains his patronymic, and is not as yet commonly called by his own name; but, although you do not know his name, I am sure that you must know his face, for that is quite enough to distinguish him.

But tell me whose son he is, I said.

He is the eldest son of Democrates, of the deme of Aexone.

Ah, Hippothales, I said; what a noble and really perfect love you have found!

(Plato, *Lysis* 203a–211a)

This dialogue (we give it here in the faded Victorian colours of Benjamin Jowett's translation) was the founding charter of a magnificent sporting institution: Baron Alphonse von Gloeden's 'Academy of Achilles' in Syracuse. Part gymnasium, part finishing-school, part tattoo-parlour, the Academy operated in this fabled Sicilian city from 1889 to 1926, offering educational opportunities to the sons of local fishermen and farmers, as well as recreation and inspiration to visiting gentlemen from the North. Seen from the outside, with its studded oak doors and ground floor of rusticated stone, it looked like a typical 18th century provincial noble's *palazzo.* Inside, it had been lovingly remodelled into an authentic recreation of an ancient Athenian gymnasium: a quadrangle with exercise yard, colonnade, undressing rooms, baths, massage couches and bowers. A place of beauty, intellect and refinement; a temple for 'the ritual sacrifice of physical energy', where minds and bodies could meet in exquisite intercourse.

For almost forty years, under the baron's punctilious command, the Academy thrived. Many a royal buttock or bicep was ornamented, in those golden years, with its miniature tattoo: a cock and trireme (symbolic of Aesculapius, god of healing, and the fleet that patrolled the Aegean). The baron himself, a bronzed, sun-worshipping Buddhist with piercing blue eyes, who remained fit and muscular well into old age, enjoyed presiding over a peculiar mix of members, of every type of social and national origin. Spanish sailors and Lithuanian truck-drivers were as welcome as French dukes.

When the *fascisti* came to power in 1922, the baron knew the game would soon be up. For the sake of his staff and friends, he kept the place open, but the old fires no longer blazed. With his strength failing, he retired to a smallholding in Kenya, where he died in December 1925. The following spring, the Academy was raided by the blackshirts. Smashed, looted and burnt, the *palazzo* and its quadrangle were bulldozed, and a large, ugly police station was erected on the site – an act of 'moral and cultural purification' of the kind that was to become unpleasantly familiar over the next fifteen years. The caretaker, Giuseppe, an old friend of the baron's, had a son in the *carabinieri*; he received a warning the day before the raid and removed key items from the office: von Gloeden's diary, a compromising photograph album, and the visitors' book – three matching volumes bound in soft turquoise leather – rich blackmail material in the wrong hands. With the help of the *carabinieri*, Giuseppe was able to ship these out to Tunis, where they passed into the hands of a Parisian book dealer, Pierre de Turckheim, whose nephew, the croupier Johnny Turckheim, very kindly showed them to us.

The passage from Plato's *Lysis* is quoted on the opening page of the baron's diary, dated 5 September, 1889. He comments:

This gives a piquant taste of the old Greek sporting scene. Men and lads at the palaistra, *posing, running, wrestling, gossiping, with nothing but a light coating of olive oil on their bodies and the joys of sport on their minds.* Homo ludens, homo felix!

After exercise, the gymnasts scrape themselves with a curved metal blade. Slaves gather the scrapers and wipe the pâté of olive oil, dust and sweat into pots, to be sold for medicinal or aphrodisiac purposes. I do not know the name of this paste but we can easily reproduce it, and must.

The athletes bathe and massage together. They watch and are watched.

Friendship is encouraged. Pederasty ('love of a

boy') is believed to be morally enriching, both for the older man who nurtures a vulnerable creature, and for the younger who gains a mentor. The boys' eyes shine with ambition for the victor's crown – but they also have a becoming modesty, for they do not know their own beauty, their complete physical perfection.

The baron was a cousin of Wilhelm von Gloeden, also of Syracuse, a classically-inspired photographer in the Uranian line. His cocky young Sicilian models stand, nonchalantly naked, next to Greek urns, or sprawl on leopardskin-draped couches. Wilhelm's exquisite silver prints of these dirty little Bacchuses were collected by princes, maharajahs, gentlemen of taste from around the world.

The von Gloedens had what the modern business world calls 'synergy'. The Academy of Achilles forged the physiques that the photographer immortalised. The boys were paid to pose. Their families were glad of the money. Everyone was happy. Over it all hovered the spirit of Eros, exactly as in ancient Greece. Kenneth Dover, in his towering monograph on *Greek Homosexuality*, explains how this worked:

The gymnasium as a whole or the wrestling-school (palaistra) *in particular provided opportunities for looking at naked boys, bringing oneself discreetly to a boy's notice in the hope of eventually speaking to him (for the gymnasium functioned as a social centre for males who could afford leisure), and even touching a boy in a suggestive way, as if by accident, while wrestling with him (cf. Plato,* Symposium 217c: *"I often wrestled with him, and no one else was there... but I didn't get any further.")*

Greek painting, on vases and elsewhere, is as graphic as Plato's dialogues. Many a hand is found on another athlete's *membrum virile,* many a *membrum* between another athlete's thighs. A red-figure cup in the Ashmolean Museum in Oxford depicts a young gentleman – bearded, muscular, lean – fondling a boy while nursing an erection worthy of an Apollo space mission. The pleasure is quite clearly mutual.

Grotesque as it may seem, there were in the days of von Gloeden, and there still are today, philistines who regard these matters as incidental to the achievements of Ancient Greece. As if that mighty flowering of scientific and creative thought had nothing to do with the culture that produced it! To these simple-minded souls we reply that two of the gymnasia in Athens were also philosophical schools: the Academy and the Lyceum, where Plato and Aristotle held court.

In homage to Baron Alphonse, we have stood bareheaded outside the Syracuse police station, remembering his life, absorbing the powerful vibrations that still emanate from the site. Inspired by his ideals, we have made the pilgrimage to Athens, city of his dreams, and walked in the sacred groves where the great thinkers taught, communing with their bright shades among the petrol fumes and klaxons of the modern city.

Having paid this tribute, we confess that beyond the enchanted world of the gymnasium we find ancient Greek sport vastly less appealing. The word 'athlete' appears to derive from the word *athlon,* meaning 'prize'. The point, apparently, was to come first. *First!* Could anything be more vulgar? More crass? It is as tedious as anything dreamed up in the fetid back rooms of American or Australian sporting clubs, where grim managers indoctrinate young men and women in the determination to win and other Hitleresque notions. We refuse to believe that Plato or Aristotle would have had anything to do with such drivel. Sport, in any civilised understanding of the word, is about play, not work.

The Greek games, it turns out, were not as innocent and light-hearted as we thought. They were jumbled with religion, tribalism, and blood-rites. One could hardly move at Olympia, it seems, for herds of cattle being driven to the altar for sacrifice, clouds of smoke from burning meat and offal, and swarms of flies. War was supposed to cease for the Games but rarely did. As the admirable Dr Spivey puts it in *The Ancient Olympics*:

> *Quite apart from the fact that the sanctuary and its lucrative festival was several times the cause of war, and the sacred precincts on at least one occasion a battleground, the whole site, including the Stadium, was decked with spoils of armed conflict. Altars were attended by specialists in sacrosanct military intelligence; events were contested to the point of serious injury and fatality; and the entire programme of athletic 'games' could be rationalised as a set of drills for cavalry and infantry fighting.*

There were redeeming features, however. Parades of naked athletes preceded the games; there was dancing in armour, torch racing, chariot-dismounting, male beauty contests – these things add a certain tone.

There was chariot-racing too, which must surely have been amusing. A spectacular and dangerous sport, it involved high-speed turns, with drivers often flung out and injured – sometimes fatally. The owners of the chariots very wisely hired slaves to do the driving, although it was always the owners, not the slaves, who won prizes. Unfairness – one of the essential ingredients of great sporting encounters – was therefore guaranteed.

Further attractions for the Decadent were the searing summer heat at Olympia, the lack of accommodation and water, poor sanitation, the constant noise of blaring trumpets, a rich tapestry of unsavoury smells, and troops of charlatans, mountebanks, philosophers, painters, astrologers, soothsayers, poets, prostitutes, thieves, and trinket-sellers. Pythagoras dropped in from Croton one year, to show off his solid gold thigh... One would have been sorry to miss that.

But let us return to the baron and his diary. He was fascinated by the subject of nakedness.

> *For aesthetic appeal it scores highly, for there is nothing in creation to match the perfection of a well-proportioned human body, as Leonardo and Michelangelo, taking up the traditions of antiquity, knew very well. But there is more to the matter than this. Ancient Mediterranean civilizations associated nudity with humiliation or transgression. When the Greeks began stripping for exercise they broke a taboo. One admires their courage. One marvels, with dear Norman Douglas (in* Siren Land*), at "the wonderful Hellenic genius for borrowing and adapting. Hermes, the intelligent thief, is a typical Greek. For whatever they stole or appropriated – religions, metals, comforts of life, architecture, engineering – they stole with exquisite taste; they discarded the dross and took only what was of value. All traces of the theft quickly vanished." But was*

it a theft? Or a borrowing? A cunning adaptation, or a bold rejection of existing customs? Pausanias writes that a sprinter called Orsippos had a half-deliberate 'accident' when his perizoma or girdle fell off during a race at Olympia in 720 BC. "He knew," says Pausanias, "that a naked man can run more easily than a man who is girt." Dionysios of Halicarnassus agrees about the date but not about the man. He says it was Akanthos the Spartan. This may seem a trivial detail, but the Spartans were the most independent-minded of the Greeks, who cared little for the opinions of others. Thucydides also votes for a Spartan origin. "They were the first," he says, "to show themselves naked in public and rub themselves with oil in sporting contests. In former days, athletes wore a sort of belt which hid their sex, even in the Olympic games."

Historians, philosophers and ethnographers speculate freely on the subject. I have read accounts which speak of "a ritual state of purity for religious purposes", a transitional stage in a rite de passage, *a form of magical protection, a relic of primitive hunting ceremonies, a homosexual predilection, a question of beauty, even a ritual of erotic self-control. I like them all. And why should they not all be valid? None excludes another.*

Personally, I favour the speed argument. It was not just a question of distance over time. Four hundred years after the winning run by Orsippos at Olympia, we find this extraordinary scene, described by Diodorus Siculus, at the camp of Alexander, on campaign in India:

Alexander recovered from his wound, sacrificed to the gods, and held a great banquet for his friends. In the

THE DECADENT SPORTSMAN

course of the drinking a curious event occurred which is worth mention. Among the king's companions there was a Macedonian named Coragus, strong in body, who had distinguished himself many times in battle. His temper was sharpened by the drink, and he challenged to single combat Dioxippus the Athenian, an athlete who had won a crown in the foremost games. As you would expect, the guests at the banquet egged them on and Dioxippus accepted. The king set a day for the contest, and when the time came, many myriads of men gathered to see the spectacle. The Macedonians and Alexander backed Coragus because he was one of them, while the Greeks favoured Dioxippus. The two advanced to the field of honour, the Macedonian clad in his expensive armour but the Athenian naked, his body oiled, carrying a well-balanced club.

Both men were fine to look upon with their magnificent physiques and their ardour for combat. Everyone looked forward, as it were, to a battle of gods. By his carriage and the brilliance of his arms, the Macedonian inspired terror as if he were Ares, while Dioxippus excelled in sheer strength and condition; still more because of his club he bore a certain resemblance to Heracles.

As they approached each other, the Macedonian flung his javelin from a proper distance, but the other inclined his body slightly and avoided its impact. Then the Macedonian poised his long lance and charged, but the Greek, when he came within reach, struck the spear with his club and shattered it. After these two defeats, Coragus was reduced to continuing the battle with his sword, but as he reached for it, the other leaped upon him and seized his swordhand with his left, while with his right the Greek upset the Macedonian's balance and made him lose his footing. As he fell to the earth, Dioxippus placed his foot upon his neck and, holding his club aloft, looked to the spectators.

The crowd was in an uproar because of the stunning quickness and superiority of the man's skill, and the king signed to let Coragus go, then broke up the gathering and left. He was plainly annoyed at the defeat of the Macedonian. Dioxippus released his fallen opponent, and left the field winner of a resounding victory and bedecked with ribands by his compatriots, as having brought a common glory to all Greeks. Fortune, however, did not allow him to boast of his victory for long.

The king continued more and more hostile to him, and Alexander's friends and all the other Macedonians about the court, jealous of the accomplishment, persuaded one of the butlers to secrete a golden cup under his pillow; then in the course of the next symposium they accused him of theft, and pretending to find the cup, placed Dioxippus in a shameful and embarrassing position. He saw that the Macedonians were in league against him and left the banquet. After a little he came to his own quarters, wrote Alexander a letter about the trick that had been played on him, gave this to his servants to take to the king, and then took his own life. He had been ill-advised to undertake the single combat, but he was much more foolish to make an end of himself in this way. Hence many of those who reviled him, mocking his folly, said that it was a hard fate to have great strength of body but little sense.

The king read the letter and was very angry at the

man's death. He often mourned his good qualities, and the man whom he had neglected when he was alive, he regretted when he was dead. After it was no longer of use, he discovered the excellence of Dioxippus by contrast with the vileness of his accusers.

The Academy of Achilles remained entirely Greek in its inspiration, avoiding what Baron Alphonse called 'the horrible sado-spectacular perversions of Rome'. By this attractive phrase he meant presumably such events as gladiator contests, naval battles, executions, combats between criminals and wild beasts.

We are not such purists as the baron. We would like to see Roman *ludi* brought into the Olympic Games. Gladiator fights and chariot-racing would, in our opinion, bring a new zest to those tired old Coubertinian rituals, stuck as they are between the aesthetics of a boy scouts' parade, a Nazi rally and a dolphin show. Corporate investors would love these enormous crowd-pleasing circuses with their thrilling brutality, their huge sales potential for television advertising. The medical sponsorship alone would make it a financial goer: think teams of doctors and paramedics rushing into the arena on motorcycles in colourful overalls to perform emergency surgery on wounded contestants, all captured on film and projected on giant screens – this could be worth $40 billion or more annually. As one City analyst put it, 'At a conservative estimate, this looks like bigger business than the destruction and rebuilding of Iraq. What's not to like?'

The Romans were no fools. By the time they conquered Greece in the mid-2nd century BC, they already knew the culture well, and treated it with respect. There were old Greek colonies in the south of Italy, cities like Croton and Syracuse whose subtle inhabitants made the Romans feel like simpletons. Greek culture was weird and cerebral, it felt like a trap. The Romans were torn between envy, disgust and fascination. As for exercising in the nude, they were appalled. The poet Ennius wrote, 'to strip in public is the beginning of evil-doing'. The Romans held fast to such feeble slogans in the hope – vain as it turned out – of avoiding corruption and moral decay.

It was not just nudity, but the entire un-military cast of the Greek approach to sport that made the Romans uncomfortable. Cicero, in his *Tusculan Disputations*, says:

> *[In our ancient laws, young men were prohibited from appearing] naked in the public baths, so far back were the principles of modesty traced by our ancestors. Among the Greeks, on the contrary, what an absurd system of training youth is exhibited in their gymnasia! What a frivolous preparation for the labours and hazards of war! What indecent spectacles, what impure and licentious amours are permitted!* (IV.iv)

Cicero's disapproval makes it all sound so much more alluring. Currents of fear and guilty attraction swirl beneath the surface. One wonders what he was afraid of.

Plutarch, in 100 AD, writes: 'The Romans are highly suspicious of rubbing with oil. They believe the main cause of the slavery and effeminacy of the Greeks is the gymnasia, which are places of idleness and pederasty in their cities.'

'Idleness and pederasty!' What a motto! It encapsulates so much. These words should be chiselled in porphyry above the doorway of every gymnasium, every office, every classroom and workshop in the land.

Despite misgivings about nudity, the Romans adored the Olympic Games, and kept them going for centuries. It was fashionable for Romans to visit Olympia and for ambitious politicians to bring Greek games to Rome. They made the athletes wear shorts, however, thus removing a large part of the attraction.

When one thinks of the glittering arc of Roman history, from the earnest dawn of Republican virtue to the purple evening of Imperial vice, it is obvious that the 'beginning of evil-doing' was not stripping in public but dark impulses deep in their own macho culture. Instead of competing amongst themselves, the Romans hired others to do it for them. They were the ultimate voyeurs, anticipating the television age. Having once been soldiers, they were drawn to the manliness of blood sports, the speed and danger of chariot-racing, which, to give them their due, they developed into vast and staggering spectacles. In all the Roman shows the slightest error could be fatal. Death was the invisible guest at the feast.

We still find the culture of Ancient Rome richly inspiring. One of our favourite Roman emperors, Heliogabalus, had deeply idiosyncratic tastes, which encompassed sado-synaesthesia and theatrical charioteering. Aelius Lampridius writes:

> *Before banquets, he used to watch gladiatorial fights and boxing-matches. He would spread a couch for himself in an upper gallery, and during the meal would arrange for a wild beast hunt with criminals... He was forever bringing four-in-hand chariots from the Circus into his dining-rooms or entrance halls while lunching*

or dining... He harnessed four huge dogs to his chariot and drove about the royal palace grounds... He also appeared in public once driving four massive stags. He harnessed lions, and declared he was the Great Mother Goddess, or tigers, when he called himself Bacchus – and he used to dress up in the costume in which the god was usually painted... His carriages were gilded or jewel-encrusted, and he scorned those that were finished in silver, ivory or bronze. He harnessed the most beautiful women in fours, or even in threes or greater numbers, to a little dog-cart, and would drive around in it, usually naked, just as the women pulling him were naked.

The gladiator shows exert a lurid magnetism. They remain as mesmerising today as they were twenty centuries ago. Why were the Romans so excited by men trying to kill each other? Why are we? Inborn sadism? A taste for brutality, cynically encouraged from above? Release of tension? Hysteria? Homophobia – killing the thing that we secretly worship? The questions echo down the tunnels of time. Cicero believed that gladiators 'taught discipline against pain and death'. Wiedemann described the arena as 'a marginal, liminal site where Romans confronted the limits of human mortality... By dying by the sword, gladiators in a sense overcame death, and their deaths provided consolation.'

Paul Plass points out that blood from dead gladiators was 'ritually poured by a high official onto a statue of Jupiter Latiaris, perhaps into its throat', although he claims that this was designed to calm the fear that the dead fighter's spirit would seek vengeance on his killers.

Despite the popularity of their shows, and the psychological service they performed, gladiators were treated badly by the citizens of Rome. In the words of Tertullian, *artem magnificant, artificem notant* – 'they admire the art, but despise the artist.' There is something painfully familiar in this tale of hypocrisy and civic ingratitude, as perhaps only those who have had a restaurant closed down by the police on grounds of 'moral hygiene' can truly understand.

In homage to the spirit of the ancient world, we perform a modest ceremony each year at the vernal equinox. Wherever we happen to be, we lock the doors, light a fire and a thurible of incense and, with the shade of that finely-tuned celebrant of antiquity David Herbert Lawrence as our invisible high priest, we strip bare for a bout of Japanese wrestling. The procedure is set out in *Women in Love,* Chapter 20:

> *'I used to do some Japanese wrestling,' said Birkin. 'A Jap lived in the same house with me in Heidelberg, and he taught me a little. But I was never much good at it.'*
>
> *'You did!' exclaimed Gerald. 'That's one of the things I've never ever seen done. You mean jiu-jitsu, I suppose?'*
>
> *'Yes. But I am no good at those things – they don't interest me.'*
>
> *'They don't? They do me. What's the start?'*
>
> *'I'll show you what I can, if you like,' said Birkin.*
>
> *'You will?' A queer, smiling look tightened Gerald's face for a moment as he said, 'Well, I'd like it very much.'*
>
> *'Then we'll try jiu-jitsu. Only you can't do much in a starched shirt.'*
>
> *'Then let us strip, and do it properly. Hold a minute –' He rang the bell and waited for the butler.*

'Bring a couple of sandwiches and a syphon,' he said to the man, 'and then don't trouble me any more tonight – or let anybody else.'

The man went. Gerald turned to Birkin with his eyes lighted.

'And you used to wrestle with a Jap?' he said. 'Did you strip?'

'Sometimes.'

'You did! What was he like then, as a wrestler?'

'Good, I believe. I am no judge. He was very quick and slippery and full of electric fire. It is a remarkable thing what a curious sort of fluid force they seem to have in them, those people – not like a human grip – like a polyp – '

Gerald nodded.

'I should imagine so,' he said, 'to look at them. They repel me, rather.'

'Repel and attract, both. They are very repulsive when they are cold, and they look grey. But when they are hot and roused, there is a definite attraction – a curious kind of full electric fluid – like eels.'

'Well – , yes – , probably.'

The man brought in the tray and set it down.

'Don't come in any more,' said Gerald.

The door closed.

'Well then,' said Gerald; 'shall we strip and begin? Will you have a drink first?'

'No, I don't want one.'

'Neither do I.'

Gerald fastened the door and pushed the furniture aside. The room was large, there was plenty of space, it was thickly carpeted. Then he quickly threw off his

THE DECADENT SPORTSMAN

clothes and waited for Birkin. The latter, white and thin, came over to him. Birkin was more a presence than a visible object; Gerald was aware of him completely, but not really visually. Whereas Gerald himself was concrete and noticeable, a piece of pure final substance.

'Now,' said Birkin, 'I will show you what I learned, and what I remember. You let me take you so – ' And his hands closed on the naked body of the other man. In another moment, he had Gerald swung over lightly and balanced against his knee, head downwards. Relaxed, Gerald sprang to his feet with eyes glittering.

'That's smart,' he said. 'Now try again.'

So the two men began to struggle together. They were very dissimilar. Birkin was tall and narrow, his bones were very thin and fine. Gerald was much heavier and more plastic. His bones were strong and round, his limbs were rounded, all his contours were beautifully and fully moulded. He seemed to stand with a proper, rich weight on the face of the earth, whilst Birkin seemed to have the centre of gravitation in his own middle. And Gerald had a rich, frictional kind of strength, rather mechanical, but sudden and invincible, whereas Birkin was abstract as to be almost intangible. He impinged invisibly upon the other man, scarcely seeming to touch him, like a garment, and then suddenly piercing in a tense fine grip that seemed to penetrate into the very quick of Gerald's being.

They stopped, they discussed methods, they practised grips and throws, they became accustomed to each other, to each other's rhythm, they got a kind of mutual physical understanding. And then again they had a real struggle. They seemed to drive their white flesh deeper and deeper against each other, as if they would break into a oneness. Birkin had a great subtle energy, that would press upon the other man with an uncanny force, weigh him like a spell put upon him. Then it would pass, and Gerald would heave free, with white, heaving, dazzling movements.

So the two men entwined and wrestled with each other, working nearer and nearer. Both were white and clear, but Gerald flushed smart red where he was touched, and Birkin remained white and tense. He seemed to penetrate into Gerald's more solid, more diffuse bulk, to interfuse his body through the body of the other, as if to bring it subtly into subjection, always seizing with some rapid necromantic fore-knowledge every motion of the other flesh, converting and counteracting it, playing upon the limbs and trunk of Gerald like some hard wind. It was as if Birkin's whole physical intelligence interpenetrated into Gerald's body, as if his fine, sublimated energy entered into the flesh of the fuller man, like some potency, casting a fine net, a prison, through the muscles into the very depths of Gerald's physical being.

So they wrestled swiftly, rapturously, intent and mindless at last, two essential white figures working into a tighter, closer oneness of struggle, with a strange, octopus-like knotting and flashing of limbs in the subdued light of the room; a tense white knot of flesh gripped in silence between the walls of old brown books. Now and again came a sharp gasp of breath, or a sound like a sigh, then the rapid thudding of movement on the thickly-carpeted floor, then the strange sound of

THE DECADENT SPORTSMAN

flesh escaping under flesh. Often, in the white interlaced knot of violent living being that swayed silently, there was no head to be seen, only the swift, tight limbs, the solid white backs, the physical junction of two bodies clinched into oneness. Then would appear the gleaming, ruffled head of Gerald, as the struggle changed, then for a moment the dun-coloured, shadowlike head of the other man would lift up from the conflict, the eyes wide and dreadful and sightless.

At length Gerald lay back inert on the carpet, his breast rising in great slow panting, whilst Birkin kneeled over him, almost unconscious. Birkin was much more exhausted. He caught little, short breaths, he could scarcely breathe any more.

The earth seemed to tilt and sway, and a complete darkness was coming over his mind. He did not know what happened. He slid forward quite unconscious over Gerald, and Gerald did not notice. Then he was half conscious again, aware only of the strange tilting and sliding of the world. The world was sliding, everything was sliding off into the darkness. And he was sliding, endlessly, endlessly away.

6

THE SCULPTOR OF FLESH

The whole art of training... consists in two things, exercise and abstinence, abstinence and exercise, repeated alternately without end. A yolk of an egg with a spoonful of rum in it is the first thing in a morning, and then a walk of six miles till breakfast. This meal consists of a plentiful supply of tea and toast and beef steaks. Then another six or seven miles till dinner-time, and another supply of solid beef or mutton with a pint of porter, and perhaps, at the utmost, a couple of glasses of sherry.
(William Hazlitt, 'The Fight', 1822)

Decadent Sportsmanship, like the Abbey of Thelema, can be approached by a multiplicity of routes. One sets out humbly, as a postulant. A non-decadent sportsman, or a non-sporting decadent. Or, conceivably, both: a couch-potato with a yearning for the body of a god. Decadence is all about transforming one's life – however sordid (in some ways the more sordid the better) – into a work of art. Decadent Sport implies a similarly visionary approach to the body.

The aesthetics of the sporting body are as fickle as the price of imperial blue tuna. There are moments in history when fashion requires the leading examples of humanity to be fat, others when they must be ascetically lean. Years of the rat, years of the hog. The 18th century in Europe was an epoch of florid rotundity; tapering off, as the century decayed, into

THE DECADENT SPORTSMAN

romantic etiolation. The 19th urbanised the consumptive look, with bony men in black suits uncannily resembling the iron and glass structures that were the architectural rage, while women shackled themselves into whalebone-stiffened dresses designed to be uncomfortable as well as sexually repellent. (Is it a coincidence that the whip became a favourite nocturnal toy?) Young Americans in 1855 were described as 'a pale, pasty-faced, narrow-chested, spindle-shanked, dwarfed race', and the average chest measurement of recruits to the British Army in 1897 was 34 inches. The Edwardian age brought back the paunch and all that went with it – the shapely buttock, the ample white breast, the trouser that gave play to the tackle within. And so the tides swung, ebbing and flooding with the moon of mode. In the past half-century America has generally required its youth to be clean-cut and athletic, with muscles racked beneath tight little T-shirts and hair slicked into Presleyan peaks. In the 1950s scrawny chaps had little chance of mating. They had sand kicked in their faces and lost their girlfriends to muscular beach bullies in scrotum-hugging briefs whose spectre has haunted the male imagination ever since.

Yet even this remarkable monotony has known its variations: a short, spectacular heyday for the skinny and unfit in the late 1960s, when beards, straggly hair, headbands, dark glasses and embroidered sheepskin coats from Afghanistan hung like old curtains from scarecrow bodies. Gymnasia became the haunts of pariahs and sweaty fanatics. 'Working out' was unheard of. Instead people were 'getting their heads together', helped by considerable inhalations of cannabis and Zen Buddhism.

Today, the athletic ideal dominates again. A new vocabulary has sprouted: everyone must be 'ripped', 'stacked', 'super-cut' or 'carved', with abdominal muscles like tank tracks, quads of steel, delts of granite and buttocks of hardboiled obsidian. There is loose talk of 'plateau busting body transformation', of 'peak physique', shock training, fat-burning, and mass-gain. Fitness programmes alternate weightlifting and cardiovascular exertion, with reps, splits, presses, crunches, thrusts, squats, curls, raises, lunges, snatches, grabs, and a thousand other postures and pistonings unmentioned in the *Kama Sutra*. These strange manoeuvres are performed in a disco-style gymnasium with brain-grinding techno music, full length mirrors and a battery-hen atmosphere. They are accompanied by a tyrannical régime of gluttony: six meals a day of egg whites, turkey breasts, cold-water fish, legumes and lean red meats – the dreariest diet imaginable – sluiced down with chocolate or banana-flavoured protein milkshakes mixed from powders shipped in plastic demijohns from Essex and Milwaukee. There is nothing remotely stylish in all this, never mind decadent. It has very little to do with sport. And yet, from these hideous routines some surprisingly elegant creatures emerge...

The transformation of the body is an ancient practice. Jockeys have lived for centuries on a diet of water, dry toast and emetics. They sweat in Turkish baths, develop phobias about food, force themselves to vomit – all in pursuit of that permanently receding ideal, a body without flesh. They want just enough muscle to get up into the saddle, drive the horse to the finish and climb off again, but not an ounce to spare. They are all bone and bad temper. Sleeping with a jockey is like a night on a pebble beach.

At the opposite extreme are the body-builders, yearning insatiably for immensity. This too is a pursuit of an ever-vanishing ideal. Once you have broken the record for the world's largest *pronator quadratus*, you have no choice but to try for the next size up. Then the one after that. It is a Holy Grail laced with poison, a chalice of flame that exacerbates the drinker's thirst – one of few such potions that we have not been tempted to drink of.

The modern cult of bulk is older than one might think. It seems to have begun in that enchanted decade which gave birth to so much that is louche, perverted and bizarre, the 1890s. Before our dear erotic pin-up Arnold Schwarzenegger there was that dark-haired angel of the posing briefs, Steve Reeves; before him Charles Atlas; and before them all a stocky little German with a rippling physique, a soft blond moustache, gentle eyes and a remarkable collection of leopardskin jockstraps: Eugene Sandow.

Sandow's early life, first in the circus, then in a touring strongman act, led to fame, wealth, sexual opportunities, and a magnificent photo-shoot for Sarony's *Living Pictures*. He wrote books, published a bodybuilding magazine, created a line of home gymnastic equipment and founded gymnasia that promised to transform millions of office clerks into the sons of Hercules. Of twenty Sandow establishments in Britain in 1900, the Institute of Physical Culture at 32A St James's Street, Piccadilly, was the luxurious headquarters. 'There were plush waiting-rooms filled with potted palms,' writes David Chapman, Sandow's biographer, 'sumptuous bathing rooms... oak-panelled smoking rooms, consulting rooms, and even a music parlour.' The exercise halls were palatial, with shining hardwood floors. A Persian carpet marked each exercise station, a set of weights racked neatly on the wall behind. Ladies had a separate gym, with curtained spaces for privacy. The first manager of the Institute was Warwick Brookes, Sandow's brother-in-law, who had been metamorphosed by the master from a delicate weakling who walked on crutches to a model of bull-like masculinity achieved through willpower and exercise alone: 'the best pupil I have ever had'. Publications such as Sandow's *Strength and How to Obtain It (1897)* and Lionel Strongfort's *Do It With Muscle!* (1924) depicted the advantages of an athletic body as well as the means to achieve it. 'Yes, faint-hearted lover,' wrote Strongfort, 'you shall very likely have her if your body is fit or when you make it so. If she seems cold to your advances a full length mirror will probably disclose the reason why.'

Sandow had discovered for himself that a well-toned physique was a powerful aphrodisiac. After his strongman show at the Trocadero Theatre in Chicago on the night of 1st August 1893, Sandow's promoter Florenz Ziegfeld announced from the footlights that any woman willing to give $300 to charity would be permitted to go backstage and feel the great man's muscles. Two wealthy ladies, Mrs Potter Palmer and Mrs George Pullman, were immediate volunteers.

In New York, an intimate post-show routine was established. After a plunge in an ice-bath, Sandow posed, spotlit, in the daintiest of briefs, among purple and black draperies, and lectured an audience of no more than fifteen on the muscles of his body. 'I want you to feel how hard these muscles are,' he would say. 'As I step before you, I want each of you to pass the palm of your hand across my chest.' A reporter from *The Police Gazette* described a girl retreating timidly as he approached. 'Never mind,' she said. 'Ah, but you must,' Sandow insisted. 'These muscles, madam, are as hard as iron itself. I want you to convince yourself of the fact.' As he passed her gloved fingers over his body she paled and faltered. 'It's unbelievable,' she murmured, and fainted into the arms of an attendant.

Developments in biochemistry since 1930 have made Sandow look sticklike. German scientists took the lead, boiling down hundreds of gallons of male urine and grinding up truckloads of testicles to produce testosterone – and, of course, to pay symbolic tribute to their fathers. Further elaborations by Nazi chemists led to industrial production. Hitler's troops were said to be dosed with steroids to increase their aggression. The Führer himself, a vegetarian hypochondriac not renowned for his physique, used them when he was feeling under-nourished. Not the best start, in public relations terms, but a reputation for magical power quickly outshone the taint of Nazi birth.

Steroids were pressed into service by postwar Russian and East German weightlifters, who grunted their way to a series of gold medals thanks to what appeared to be superhuman strength. In 1958 Dianabol was approved for sale in the USA, and this strange alchemy was released into the Free World. Medical uses were followed by sporting abuse. Athletes complained of prostate enlargement and shrunken testicles. The International Olympic Committee banned steroids in 1976. But there is nothing like a ban to increase sales, and the drugs are now available to athletes in the form of injectable solutions, pills, creams and patches, through mail order (in plain, unmarked packaging) and personal suppliers. The frontiers of body change have been magnificently expanded. Bodybuilders of the past few decades have been able to cut themselves free of medical advice, the survival instinct, even their own physical reactions, to develop bloated physiques that are the stuff of nightmares – Incredible Hulks assembled from roasted blood sausage, inflated to 400 pounds per square inch, cabled with clenched fibres, and smeared with tanning oil.

Steve Michalik was a glittering example of the genre. His titles (Mr Apollo, Mr America, Mr Universe, Most Muscular Man in the USA, etc) give no hint of the sinister king-cobra thorax and the venom he absorbed to achieve it. In a 1990 article in *The Village Voice* ('The Power and the Gory'), Paul Solotaroff told the heroic tale, in suitably pumped style, of a man who sacrificed everything to get to the top:

> *For himself, Michalik only wanted two things anymore. He wanted to walk on stage at the Beacon Theater on November 15, 1986, professional bodybuilding's Night of Champions, and just turn the joint out with his 260 pounds of ripped, stripped, and shrink-wrapped muscle. And then, God help him, he wanted to die. Right there in front of everybody, with all the flash bulbs popping, he wanted to drop dead huge and hard at the age of thirty-nine, and leave a spectacular corpse behind.*
>
> *The pain, you see, had become just unendurable. Ten years of shotgunning steroids had turned his joints into fish jelly, and spiked his blood pressure so high he had to pack his nose to stop the bleeding. He'd been pissing blood for months, and what was coming out of him now was brown, pure protoplasm that his engorged liver hadn't the wherewithal to break down. And when he came home from the gym at night, his whole body was in spasm. His eight year old boy, Steve junior, had to pack his skull in ice, trying to take the top 10 percent off his perpetual migraine.*
>
> *"I knew it was all over for me," Michalik says. "Every system in my body was shot, my testicles had shrunk to the size of cocktail peanuts. It was only a*

question of which organ was going to explode on me first.

"See, we'd all of us been way over the line for years, and it was like, suddenly all the bills were coming in. Victor Faizowitz took so much shit that his brain exploded. The Aldactazone sent his body temperature up to one hundred twelve degrees, and he literally melted to death. Another guy, an Egyptian bodybuilder training for the Mr Universe contest, went the same way, a massive haemorrhage from head to toe – died bleeding out of every orifice. And Tommy Sansone, a former Mr America who'd been my very first mentor in the gym, blew out his immune system on Anadrol and D-ball and died of tumors all over his body.

"As for me I couldn't wait to join 'em. I had so much evil in me from all the drugs I was taking that I'd go home at night and ask God why he hadn't killed me yet. And then, in the next breath, I'd say 'Please, I know I've done a lot of terrible things – sold steroids to kids, beaten the shit out of strangers – but please don't let me go out like a sucker, God. Please let me die hitting that last pose at the Beacon with the crowd on its feet for a second standing O.'"

Michalik's prayers might better have been addressed to a liver specialist.

Paul Solotaroff knew what he was talking about. In *The Body Shop: Parties, Pills, and Pumping Iron – or, My Life in the Age of Muscle* he reveals that he too had spent time injecting his buttocks with anabolic steroids. The son of Ted Solotaroff, a New York intellectual, Paul began bodybuilding in the hope of 're-architecturing' his body and increasing his sex-appeal.

THE DECADENT SPORTSMAN

His brother Ivan remembers Paul having only two household possessions at the time: a suitcase full of disco clothes and a blender for protein shakes. With the help of steroids and a ferocious weightlifting programme he picked up a plethora of chicks – and life-threatening ailments. 'All around the country,' Steve Michalik had said, 'kids'll be dropping dead from the stuff, and getting diabetes because it burns out their pancreas. I don't care what those assholes in California say, there's no such thing in the world as a 'good' drug. There's only bad drugs and sick bastards who want to sell them to you.'

As Decadent Sportsmen we can only admire the grotesque physical results achieved by the bodybuilders. There is something heroic, as well as intensely foolish, in their endeavours. At the same time the effort and tedium involved in all that weightlifting, the clanking of machinery, the grimacing, the clenching, the plunging of syringes into buttocks, not least the vulgarity of the clothing and what appears to be a compulsory stupidity in its practitioners, exclude it as a sport for the Decadent. We prefer to study the older training and diet systems.

The Spartans trained both boys and girls, bringing them to a pitch of physical toughness that would equip them handsomely for battlefield and bedroom. Boys were grouped by age into *agelai* or herds, supervised by older boys and a *paidonomos* or magistrate who took charge of their education. A poor diet developed their foraging skills. Rough games and competitive exercise encouraged manliness, agility, and strength. There were public displays of naked young manhood, with contests, parades and rituals such as the Hyakinthia and the Karneia, with music, dancing and grape-running. Spartan youths were scrupulously inspected every ten days by a magistrate; if they were fit they were praised, if not they were flogged. In this men's club atmosphere, the state smiled benignly on homoerotic and pederastic relationships. Anyone who has attended a British boarding school will recognise the pattern immediately. It is most refreshing to reflect that Baron de Coubertin, the founder of the modern Olympics, was as inspired by the English public-school sporting ideal as he was by the Greek.

'Only chariot drivers and jockeys could be clothed,' writes Donald Kyle. 'All competitors in the stadium were nude – no jockstrap, no shoes, no place for endorsements, just a thin coat of olive oil.' As H. A. Harris points out in his masterly *Greek Athletes and Athletics,* there were 'three Greek words for trainer, *paidotribēs, aleiptēs and gymnastēs...* The literal meaning of *paidotribēs,* 'boy-rubber', and *aleiptēs,* 'anointer', suggests that massage was an important part of their duties.'

About 500 B.C. Greek athletes switched from a diet of soft cheese and figs to a heavy meat intake. In this they are said (by Plutarch) to have been led by Pythagoras, although the great man himself was a vegetarian. Milo of Croton seems a more likely model. Legendary for his size, strength and appetite, this 6th century wrestler was champion seven times at Delphi, ten at Isthmia, nine at Nemea. His eating alone would have earned him a place in the record books: twenty pounds of meat, twenty of bread, and eight quarts of wine on one occasion. On another he carried a four-year old bull the length of the stadium, then butchered and ate the whole beast in a single day. Like many a star he had eccentric beliefs. He attributed his invincibility to eating the gizzard-stones of cockerels.

There were excesses, then as now. Euripides called athletes 'the slaves of their jaws and the victims of their bellies', and Philostratus, a century later, ridiculed coaches who 'solemnly discussed the relative merits for a training diet of deep-sea and inshore fish, basing their arguments on the kind of seaweed each was likely to have eaten.' His ridicule seems harsh. Athletes' bodies are finely-tuned engines. They must have the right fuel, or they will run badly. Decadent athletes are even more sensitive; theirs must be a gourmet diet, prepared by the finest chefs using rare and exquisite ingredients.

For the true Decadent Sportsman the person to turn to for advice is the Divine Marquis. De Sade himself had a rather sweet tooth. His letters to his wife from the prison of Vincennes in the 1780s are full of desperate pleas for 'four dozen meringues, two dozen sponge cakes and four dozen chocolatines – with vanilla.' Plenty of quick-burn energy there, but little in the way of stamina food. For the libertines whom he conjures into life in his books, their training regimes are rather more varied and substantial. After all, they undertake lengthy physical activity which can certainly take it out of them, so to speak. In *La Nouvelle Justine*, as a prelude to debauchery, the Comte de Gernande sits down to a banquet which comprises:

> *...two soup dishes, one of Italian pasta with saffron, the other a bisque au coulis de jambon and between them, a plate of veal steaks à l'anglaise. Twelve hors d'oeuvres followed: six cooked, six raw. Then there were twelve main dishes; four of meat, four of game and four of pies. A boar's head was served surrounded by twelve plates of roast meat, accompanied by two servings of garnish, six of vegetables, six different sauces and six of pies. These were followed by twenty plates of fruit or compotes, an assortment of six ices, eight different wines, six liqueurs, rum, punch, cinnamon liqueurs, chocolate and coffee.*

In addition, Gernande consumes:

> ...four bottles of Volnay, before moving on to four Ais with the roast meat. He made short shrift of a bottle of Tokay, a Paphos, a Madeira and a Falerno with the fruit, and he finished up with two bottles of liqueur des îles, a pint of rum, two glasses of punch and ten cups of coffee.

This may not be the ideal pre-match build-up for all athletes, but at least it is not as heavy as the meal Minski the Muscovite giant places in front of Juliette and her companions at his castle in Italy. Minski's is a simple meat diet, which would be approved of by those trophological nutritionists who warn that the mixing of carbohydrate-rich foods and protein-rich foods in the same meal can be detrimental to health. Minski's meal consists of more than twenty entrées and roast dishes, washed down with thirty bottles of wine of various sorts. Mid-course, Minski announces to his guests that all the meat before them is human flesh and he provides a not unconvincing argument in favour of cannibalism. He also claims that his diet is the reason he is capable of ejaculating ten times a day without suffering from the slightest fatigue. "Whoever tries this diet," he announces. "will certainly increase threefold their libidinous faculties, to say nothing of the strength, health and youthfulness that this food will develop in you." A ringing endorsement.

Our understanding of the role of diet in training has come a long way since the Divine Marquis, however. Thanks to advances in the science of nutrition we can propose a much more balanced programme, such as this decadent sporting regimen for today, drawn up for us by Ronnie 'the Pope'

THE DECADENT SPORTSMAN

Mascareñas, Chief Fitness and Muscle Engineer in the Old Havana Boxing Gymnasium. He calls it The Gladiator-Maker.

10.30 am BREAKFAST
Half a dozen blood oranges blended with a dozen oysters at 2500 rpm (45 seconds).

11.00 am IRIS ROUTINE (ICE, RUB, INGEST & SOAK)
Stage 1: plunge into ice bath – full submersion (3 minutes)
Stage 2: rub down with sesame and eucalyptus oils spiked with arnica (sesame for burning fat; eucalyptus for cleaning the airways; arnica for bruising)
Stage 3: soak in milk bath and drink two cups of coffee:

Coffee 1: 'Soviet Wrestler' blend double espresso (Don Mayo Especial, Costa Rica) with extracts of fenugreek, maca root, tribulus terrestris, longjack root, saw palmetto, shiitake mushroom, garlic and ginger.
Coffee 2: Los Placeres, Nicaragua, hot-pressed through raw silk.

11.30 am TRAINING
30 minutes each on punch bag, weights, running track.

1.00 pm LUNCH
Steak, eggs, avocado, asparagus.
Pineapple and pomegranate.

2.00–5.00 pm SIESTA

THE DECADENT SPORTSMAN

5.00 pm TEA
Rose Pouchong or Formosa Oolong.
Dundee cake spiked with zinc, magnesium, vitamin B6.

5.30 pm TRAINING
Jog down to the beach and horse around in the water for half an hour.
Volleyball, touch rugby, gymnastics.
Another swim.

7.00 pm MASSAGE
Olive oil and a 'boy-rubber'

7.30 pm TIFFIN
Caviar, sushi and samphire club sandwich, with a tumbler of iced white rum.

8.00 pm SPIRITUAL TRAINING
Baudelaire, *Les Fleurs du mal*

8.45 pm EVENING FEAST
One whole goat, with root vegetables.
Château Pétrus.

NOCTURNAL IRIS ROUTINE
As above (11.00 am) but with schnapps instead of coffee.

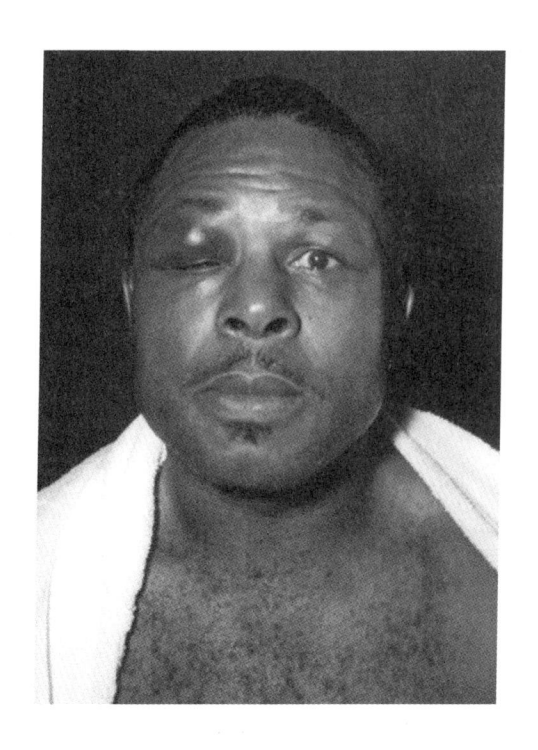

7

THE FIGHTER

Hounded by police and harassed by debt-collectors, we have found an anchorage at last in an enfilade of first-floor rooms at El Periquito, a cabaret-brothel in Old Havana. A home of sorts in this shifting world, it remains our haven, our Parnassus, our *petit paradis terrestre*. Along the creaking corridor, whores and rent-boys ply their ancient trade. The walls of their bedchambers are faded pink, the carpets threadbare, the furniture upholstered in the balding hides of leopards and zebras. Groans of release can be heard through the plasterboard partitions as long-distance truck drivers, sailors and aircrew are catapulted luxuriously into $35 worth of nirvana.

Señora Carmela runs the business from her saloon at the top of the stairs. Like a Caribbean Catherine the Great, she sits enthroned at a table draped in crimson velvet, with five ritual objects to hand: a black leather notebook, a silver pencil, a vase of paper roses, a glass of crème de menthe, and an old Cuban army revolver. Once a month she steps out into the yard with the revolver to shoot the necks off a row of bottles. The mere presence of the weapon wards off unwanted customers, while the crème de menthe has a similarly apotropaic effect on the pox.

The ground floor is rented out to the Gimnaseo de Boxeo Guillermo Horta, a popular sporting institution founded in the late 1950s by a retired Olympic boxer and nightclub owner, who, after a waterskiing accident and an ecstatic therapeutic vision of the Virgin Mary, devoted his life to the education and redemption of slum boys. It is a spartan place, redolent of canvas, rope, male sweat, varnished wood, and menthol muscle-rub. We like the gym very much. Our fascination with its workings has flowered like a tropical hibiscus. We have taken to hanging out among the boxers, getting to know the trainers and the lads who come in every afternoon to lift weights, strike punchbags and spar in outsize gloves – poor black and mestizo boys hungry for muscle and respect.

There is something erotic in their bruising. Something fertile and lurid. We feel perfectly at home. We ask no questions, and none are asked of us. On these hot, airless Havana afternoons, strange ideas are born. One such was the notion that we might rise from our lethargy and become fit, exchanging the torpor of the *chaise longue* for the tempests and high colours of the boxing ring.

We have always enjoyed a good fight. We love the tension, the excitement, the blue steel of unsheathed claws – not to mention the violent beauty of all combat.

The roots of man-to-man fighting lie twisted deep in the past. Well-oiled musclemen hitting each other has long been acknowledged as a crowd-puller. The Babylonians liked nothing better. The Cretans, Egyptians and Sumerians were fierce addicts. Here is the *Epic of Gilgamesh*:

Enkidu blocked the doorway with his foot.
They grappled,
crouching like wrestlers.
They smashed the doorpost,
the walls trembled...

It's a scene which we read with a shudder of recognition, so vividly does it remind us of the kitchen of the Decadent

Restaurant. We had fights in there practically every night – our guests adored it. A new edge was brought to the pleasures of the table by sudden eruptions of shouting and smashing of plates behind swing doors.

Certain occasions stand out in the memory. Vasily, a chef from Georgia, once drew a handgun – a vicious little Esser & Schmidt with five rubies in the handle – and aimed an angry volley at Serge, the head waiter, who had accused him of being too drunk to cook. Serge was absolutely right: Vasily was not only too drunk to cook but also too drunk to shoot straight. Having emptied the magazine he fell over, striking his head on a butcher's block as he went down. There was blood, but it was all his own.

Of course spilt blood means ambulances, police, awkward questions (irritations unknown to the ancient Sumerians). We therefore decided to limit the staff to fist fights – which was a great improvement. Call it sentimental, but we find there is much to be said for the weapons code of the old East End of London, in the palmy days before the Kray twins moved in and began executing their rivals with twelve-bores. 'Shooters' were, until then, regarded as the height of vulgarity. Knives were for nancies. If you couldn't punch your way out of trouble, the East Enders used to say, you should never have been in it in the first place.

Kitchens are a natural arena for punch-ups, but the dining room is unquestionably more elegant. A number of the more louche Roman emperors (Caligula, Nero, Commodus, Heliogabalus) took special pleasure in viewing gladiator fights from their banqueting tables. The grunts, the smells, the spurt and splash of blood would certainly have helped to whet their coarse appetites.

Having established the principle of *la bagarre dans la salle à manger,* it remains to choose the precise form of combat to accompany the particular occasion. This is a delicate matter, on which one cannot spend too much time and thought.

A good all-purpose dinner-fight is the old Greek *pankration*, which had just three rules: fight like hell, and no biting or eye-gouging. Everything else was permitted: punching, kicking, stamping, chopping, jabbing, twisting, tripping, head-butting, kneeing, crushing, throttling, wrenching, ripping, bludgeoning, even abusing the opponent's testicles in a variety of colourful ways – in fact the full range of manly violence. There is an honesty about *pankration*. A directness. A masculinity. It stimulates the digestive fluids remarkably.

Pankration can be lethal, however. In one legendary contest at Nemea, which failed to reach a conclusion by sunset, the combatants were stopped and given the chance to inflict a single final blow. Pausanias writes:

> *Kreugas threw his punch at Damoxenos' head. Then Damoxenos told Kreugas to raise his arm, and jabbed him under the ribs with his fingers straight. His sharp nails and the force of the blow drove his hand into Kreugas' guts. He seized Kreugas' intestines and ripped them out. Kreugas died on the spot.*

This kind of thing, unless properly handled, can put people off their food. Use a little imagination, however, and it offers a perfect opportunity for culinary theatre. With a hot grill nearby, the losing pankratiatist's intestines can be served as *Saucisses à la Kreugas*. Few guests will forget the scene.

For an outdoor occasion, a picnic or *fête champêtre,* one can scarcely improve on a mediaeval joust, with knights in iron suits lumbering towards each other on horseback, greaves clanking, vambraces squeaking, gorgets rattling, hauberks tinkling, lances phallically cocked, while the ladies wave silken banners of devotion and shriek with excitement in the hospitality pavilions. Trumpets blare. Shawms fart. Steel clashes with steel. Armoured bodies thud to the ground. It's crude and titanically virile. Spectators are of course denied the sight of glistening muscles, but the imagination offers its own delights. Somewhere under all those layers of armour plate, chain mail and sweat-soaked padding there must lurk a fine specimen of manhood. Like the racing drivers of today, sheathed in their hideous fire-suits, these are invisible men.

For an urban picnic, we favour swordplay in the *Romeo and Juliet*-style, with a pair of *bravi* in tights and open-fronted white shirts, a dagger in one hand, a sword in the other, and a serious intention to draw blood. Pistol shooting is an alternative, and there is virtually no limit on the weapons that might be used, from the mediaeval stave to the contemporary bazooka.

More naked, more brutal, and an infallible crowd-pleaser, is bare-knuckle boxing. This works in any context, but best on the large scale – the gala banquet, the big-ticket birthday celebration, the Pompeiian feast. Boxing blossomed in the magic world of eighteenth century England – a Garden of Eden in history more luxuriantly fertile even than Ancient Olympia, a place where all Decadents feel instinctively at home. In that enchanted nook of time, horse-racing, cock-fighting, coursing with hares, cricket, boxing and fox-hunting spread like a bushfire through the shires of England, fanned by spice-laden winds from the East and West Indies, blasted by the hot breath of the industrial revolution. Not since the crumbling of the amphitheatres and the rusting of gladiatorial swords had the plebeian hordes swarmed to the contest in such vast and drunken numbers. A sport-loving class – 'the Fancy' – flourished in province and city. Rakes, parsons, lords, tradesmen, pimps, chancers, apprentices, a lavish social mélange, indulged their ludic passions at every opportunity; and inflamed them with the most exhilarating sport of all – gambling.

In this glittering arena, boxing – 'the noble art' – flourished anew. It drew vast crowds. Men fought stripped to the waist, wearing breeches and stockings but no gloves. In encounters of primeval brutality, lips were split, noses crushed, eyes swollen, jaws broken, wrists and fingers smashed. Blood, referred to as 'claret', flowed freely. A bout might last two hours or more, ending at the point when one contestant was too exhausted to stand up. There were no 'rounds', no pauses in the fighting, until Jack Broughton introduced a set of rules in 1743, allowing thirty seconds' recovery to a man who had been knocked down, with a further eight seconds to 'come to the scratch'.

The essential principles of boxing are laid out in an 18th century text, 'Canons of Pugilism':

From the time of the first man, *the hand of brother hath been lifted against brother;*
sometimes aided with instruments – missiles;
but the fists *are the only* arms *nature supplies.*
This is the only true *and* natural *mode of FIGHTING:*
all others being brutal – assassin-like;
it belongs wholly to the realms of Britain,
and is practised most scientifically in the metropolis.
Certain points (or parts) of man are vital; for, being hit hard,
this produceth apoplexy, rupture, blindness, death.
These points are – the pit of the stomach, (or Broughton's mark);

THE DECADENT SPORTSMAN

the lowest rib, or liver-hit – vulgo, *the kidney;*
the neck, or jugular – affecting the brain;
the eyes, ears, and whisker-hit.
To prevent those unhappy consequences, all men learn the art of
defending the points.

Prize fights were illegal but attracted thousands to the lonely country spots where they were held. Pierce Egan describes the scene in Newbury on 11 December 1821 as the London Fancy passed through on their way to Hungerford Down for a big match:

Tuesday morning, long before the darkey had brushed away, presented a nouvelle scene to the Johnny Raws, by the numerous arrivals of the amateurs from London, who had been on the road all night, with their peepers half open, and their tits [horses] almost at a stand-still. About ten o'clock, Newbury presented an interesting appearance. The inhabitants were all out of their doors; the windows of the houses crowded with females, anxiously waiting to witness the departure of the Fancy to the mill. Indeed, it was a lively picture to see, in rapid motion, barouches and fours, curricles, post-chaises, gigs, carts, stage-coaches, waggons, myriads of yokels on horseback, chaw-bacons scampering along the road, Corinthians and bang-up lads showing their gallantry to the lovely fair ones, as they passed along, which were returned by nods and smiles, indicating that "none but the brave deserve the fair".

Bill Neate, a six-foot butcher from Bristol, had challenged Tom Hickman, the Champion of England, known as 'the Gas-man'.

THE DECADENT SPORTSMAN

25,000 people watched the match, including William Hazlitt, who left his own description of the proceedings in a piece called *The Fight*. Hazlitt had left London the previous afternoon in a coach, and travelled all night, chatting and drinking with his companions of the road, assessing the chances of the Bristol butcher against 'the Gas-man'. Arriving at Newbury at seven in the morning, they refreshed themselves with a few drinks, then walked the nine miles to Hungerford.

> *The day was fine, the sky was blue, the mists were retiring from the marshy ground, the path was tolerably dry, the sitting-up all night had not done us much harm – at least the cause was good; we talked of this and that with amicable difference, roving and sipping of many subjects, but still invariably we returned to the fight. At length, a mile to the left of Hungerford, on a gentle eminence, we saw the ring surrounded by covered carts, gigs, and carriages, of which hundreds had passed us on the road; Tom gave a youthful shout, and we hastened down a narrow lane to the scene of action.*
>
> *Reader, have you ever seen a fight? If not, you have a pleasure to come, at least if it is a fight like that between the Gas-man and Bill Neate. The crowd was very great when we arrived on the spot; open carriages were coming up, with streamers flying and music playing, and the country-people were pouring in over hedge and ditch in all directions, to see their hero beat or be beaten.*

The odds, which they checked as soon as they arrived, were still on Hickman, but only about five to four. Around £200,000 was at stake.

The grass was wet, and the ground miry, and ploughed up with multitudinous feet, except that, within the ring itself, there was a spot of virgin-green closed in and unprofaned by vulgar tread, that shone with dazzling brightness in the mid-day sun. For it was noon now, and we had an hour to wait. This is the trying time. It is then the heart sickens, as you think what the two champions are about, and how short a time will determine their fate. After the first blow is struck, there is no opportunity for nervous apprehensions; you are swallowed up in the immediate interest of the scene – but

>   *Between the acting of a dreadful thing*
>   *And the first motion, all the interim is*
>   *Like a phantasma, or a hideous dream.*

I found it so as I felt the sun's rays clinging to my back, and saw the white wintry clouds sink below the verge of the horizon. "So," I thought, "my fairest hopes have faded from my side! – so will the Gas-man's glory, or that of his adversary, vanish in an hour."

The swells were parading in their white box-coats, the outer ring was cleared with some bruises on the heads and shins of the rustic assembly (for the cockneys had been distanced by the sixty-six miles); the time drew near, I had got a good stand; a bustle, a buzz, ran through the crowd, and from the opposite side entered Neate, between his second and bottle-holder. He rolled along, swathed in his loose great coat, his knock-knees bending under his huge bulk; and, with a modest cheerful air, threw his hat into the ring. He then just looked round, and began quietly to undress; when from the other side there was a similar rush and an opening made, and the Gas-man came forward with a conscious air of anticipated triumph, too much like the cock-of-the-walk. He strutted about more than became a hero, sucked oranges with a supercilious air, and threw away the skin with a toss of his head, and went up and looked at Neate, which was an act of supererogation. The only sensible thing he did was, as he strode away from the modern Ajax, to fling out his arms, as if he wanted to try whether they would do their work that day. By this time they had stripped, and presented a strong contrast in appearance. If Neate was like Ajax, "with Atlantean shoulders, fit to bear" the pugilistic reputation of all Bristol, Hickman might be compared to Diomed, light, vigorous, elastic, and his back glistened in the sun, as he moved about, like a panther's hide.

There was now a dead pause – attention was awe-struck. Who at that moment, big with a great event, did not draw his breath short – did not feel his heart throb? All was ready. They tossed up for the sun, and the Gas-man won. They were led up to the scratch – shook hands, and went at it.

In the first round everyone thought it was all over. After making play a short time, the Gas-man flew at his adversary like a tiger, struck five blows in as many seconds, three first, and then following him as he staggered back, two more, right and left, and down he fell, a mighty ruin. There was a shout, and I said, "There is no standing this." Neate seemed like a lifeless lump of flesh and bone, round which the Gas-man's blows played with the rapidity of electricity or lighting, and you imagined he would only be lifted up to be knocked down again. It was as if Hickman held a sword or a fire in the right hand of his, and directed it against an unarmed body. They met again, and Neate seemed, not cowed, but particularly cautious. I saw his teeth clenched together and his brows knit close against the sun. He held out both his arms at full-length straight before him, like two sledge-hammers, and raised his left an inch or two higher. The Gas-man could not get over this guard – they struck mutually and fell, but without advantage on either side. It was the same in the next round; but the balance of power was thus restored – the fate of the battle was suspended. No one could tell how it would end.

This was the only moment in which opinion was divided; for, in the next, the Gas-man aiming a mortal blow at his adversary's neck, with his right hand, and failing from the length he had to reach, the other returned it with his left at full swing, planted a tremendous blow on his cheek-bone and eyebrow, and made a red ruin of that side of his face. The Gas-man went down, and there was another shout – a roar of triumph as the waves of fortune rolled tumultuously from side to side. This was a settler. Hickman got up, and "grinned horrible a ghastly smile," yet he was evidently dashed in his opinion of himself; it was the first time he had ever been so punished; all one side of his face was perfect scarlet, and his right eye was closed in dingy blackness, as he advanced to the fight, less confident, but still determined. After one or two rounds, not receiving another such remembrancer, he rallied and went at it with his former impetuosity. But

> *in vain. His strength had been weakened – his blows could not tell at such a distance – he was obliged to fling himself at his adversary, and could not strike from his feet; and almost as regularly as he flew at him with his right hand, Neate warded the blow, or drew back out of its reach, and felled him with the return of his left. There was little cautious sparring – no half-hits – no tapping and trifling, none of the* petit-maîtreship *of the art – they were almost all knock-down blows: – the fight was a good stand-up fight.*

We are offended by this slighting reference to *petit-maîtreship* – it is already a huge step for a Decadent to enter the boxing ring, and 'tapping and trifling' are very much the upper limit for anyone who cares for his appearance – but, despite a shiver of aesthetic revulsion, one can share Hazlitt's admiration of the fighters' endurance:

> *The wonder was the half-minute time. If there had been a minute or more allowed between each round, it would have been intelligible how they should by degrees recover strength and resolution; but to see two men smashed to the ground, smeared with gore, stunned, senseless, the breath beaten out of their bodies; and then, before you recover from the shock, to see them rise up with new strength and courage, stand steady to inflict or receive mortal offence, and rush upon each other, "like two clouds over the Caspian" – this is the most astonishing thing of all: – this is the high and heroic state of man!*

Even heroes, however, must fade, no matter how strongly

built. The fight begins to turn:

> *From this time forward the event became more certain every round; and about the twelfth it seemed as if it must have been over. Hickman generally stood with his back to me; but in the scuffle, he had changed positions, and Neate just then made a tremendous lunge at him, and hit him full in the face. It was doubtful whether he would fall backwards or forwards; he hung suspended for about a second or two, and then fell back, throwing his hands in the air, and with his face lifted up to the sky. I never saw anything more terrific than his aspect just before he fell. All traces of life, of natural expression, were gone from him. His face was like a human skull, a death's head, spouting blood. The eyes were filled with blood, the nose streamed with blood, the mouth gaped blood. He was not like an actual man, but like a preternatural, spectral appearance, or like one of the figures in Dante's "Inferno." Yet he fought on after this for several rounds, still striking the first desperate blow, and Neate standing on the defensive, and using the same cautious guard to the last, as if he had still all his work to do; and it was not till the Gas-man was so stunned in the seventeenth or eighteenth round, that his senses forsook him, and he could not come to time, that the battle was declared over.*

We admire the gothic grotesqueness of the Gas-man's transformation, painted not with make-up but with his own blood. There is something of the Body Artist in Mr Hickman, a foretaste of those great self-mutilators of the 1960s, Rudolf Schwarzkogler and Günter Brus... But of course Hazlitt too is in the business of converting violence into art. He stresses the courage of the contestants once again, and then their good manners:

Ye who despise the FANCY, do something to show as much pluck, or as much self-possession as this, before you assume a superiority which you have never given a single proof of by any one action in the whole course of your lives! – When the Gas-man came to himself, the first words he uttered were, "Where am I? What is the matter!" "Nothing is the matter, Tom – you have lost the battle, but you are the bravest man alive." And Jackson whispered to him, "I am collecting a purse for you, Tom." – Vain sounds, and unheard at that moment!

Neate instantly went up and shook him cordially by the hand, and seeing some old acquaintance, began to flourish with his fists, calling out, "Ah, you always said I couldn't fight – What do you think now?" But all in good humour, and without any appearance of arrogance; only it was evident Bill Neate was pleased that he had won the fight. When it was all over, I asked Cribb if he did not think it was a good one? He said, "Pretty well!" The carrier-pigeons now mounted into the air, and one of them flew with the news of her husband's victory to the bosom of Mrs. Neate. Alas, for Mrs. Hickman!

There is no reason, of course, why a bare-knuckle fight should be restricted to full-grown men. Boys can be just as entertaining. The Reverend C. Allix Wilkinson, in his *Reminiscences of Eton* (1888) devotes a chapter to this subject, beginning on a stirring note:

Fighting! What will the mammas say to this?
 I remember a near relation of mine coming to see me with a letter in her hand and her eyes streaming with tears, the first news she had received from her dear, delicate, beautiful first-born. He had not been at Eton a week, and he had had a fight and had two black eyes. 'I am uncommonly glad to hear it,' was my cruel answer; 'it shows his pluck.'

The parson continues in this vein, quoting the Duke of Wellington ('our battle-ground was the playing-fields') and speaking with disrespect of those 'who are content to live as idle, useless, isolated items in the busy world, as if they had no part to play and nothing to do but to eat, drink, and amuse themselves.'

The Rev's confusion deepens as he tells the tale of Ashley, a 'kind, jolly, curly-headed youngster', who fought a bigger boy one evening, watched by a large crowd.

Both were fighting like professionals of the ring, stripped naked to the waist, the bottle-holders on both sides cheering on their respective champions. Unfortunately, the bottles contained brandy, which had been given with thoughtless but good intentions, though, it was said at the inquest, with fatal effect. But no one could really blame the seconds. They wished to keep their exhausted friends till ten minutes before lock-up was called, and then they must conclude and shake hands.
 I believe there was only one minute to fight when the last blow was given, and poor little Ashley fell senseless

and never spoke again. I saw him carried in naked to the waist on the shoulders of four boys – we all said, 'poor fellow, he is gone,' as the bell rang for absence and the doors of the two houses were closed. The doctor had been of course sent for, and within half-an-hour we heard from our window some heartrending sobs; we looked out and could distinguish in the closing darkness his poor brother in the yard wringing his hands, and to our question he said, 'The doctor has been. It is too true – the dear fellow is dead!'

The depression in the school was indescribable.

Dr Keate, the head master, addressed the boys, stating, 'It is not that I object to fighting in itself; on the contrary, I like to see a boy who receives a blow return it at once, but that you, the heads of the school, should allow a contest to go on for two hours and a half, has shocked and grieved me.' He urged the boys to act with better judgement in future, and 'under a deeper sense of responsibility'.

Our philosophical narrator finds that 'good undoubtedly came out of this sad evil': the boys were 'fully impressed' with Keate's words. They continued to fight, of course, 'but always after dinner'.

The Decadent Sportsman may console himself with the thought that he would have been much too busy being 'idle, useless and isolated', or perhaps 'eating, drinking and amusing himself' to have witnessed this sorry scene.

Meanwhile in China... Throughout the 18th and 19th centuries there were Buddhist and Taoist sects who appropriated martial arts to form protest and liberation movements. In the late 1890s, a new participation sport was spreading through northwest Shantung province 'like a whirlwind'. Followers of a sect known as the Spirit Boxers set up boxing grounds in temple precincts. Chanting spells and inviting the gods to possess them, they entered a trance, which turned to a whirling, dancing frenzy as the god moved in, supposedly making them invulnerable to bullets, swords, arrows and blows. 'Public demonstrations of the boxers' invulnerability were frequent,' writes Peter Fleming in *The Siege at Peking.* 'The audiences were large, and seem never to have been disappointed. Sword-cuts and pike-thrusts were seen to make no impression on bodies which the spirits had entered; bullets were deflected by a wave of the hand.' The spectators were peasants, easily impressed. When the boxers suffered injuries the credulous viewers accepted the most specious explanations. Fleming continues: 'Accidents were, inevitably, caused by failures in the chicanery and legerdemain without which these tests must have proved either unconvincing to the audience or fatal to the actors; one keen fellow had the ill luck to be blown in two by a cannon-ball. But these miscarriages were glossed over by explaining that their victims had been lax in performing their devotions or had transgressed one of the numerous bye-laws of the Society.' The Spirit Boxers quickly gathered followers. Their heirs were the I Ho Tuan, or Boxers United in Righteousness, who, with the blessing of the Dowager Empress T'zu Hsi, slaughtered missionaries and other foreign residents in the Boxer Rebellion of 1899–1900.

Collectors of ritual that we are, we note the following description from the American scholar J.W. Esherick, on page 218 of his *Origins of the Boxer Uprising*:

The standard format for the possession ritual involved kowtowing to the southeast, burning incense, and performing a simple purification ritual of drinking clear water. Then the boxer would usually sit on a chair on top of a table, and call upon his "teacher" to "come down from the mountain" (qing lao-shi xia-shan). With his eyes closed, the boxer would slowly go into a trance, begin wavering about and breathing rapidly until he finally went into a frenzy of possession by his god. Each boxer would be possessed by a particular god, and that god would, in effect, become part of the individual's identity. Virtually without exception, the possessing gods were the heroes of popular literature and theatre.

An amusing variation on the classic boxing-match is to pit an exceptionally capable fighter against one who has barely any idea what he is doing. Naturally there are people who will object to this, on the grounds that (a) it is a waste of a decent boxer's time, and (b) betting becomes pointless since the outcome is a foregone conclusion. But things do not always work out exactly as expected. Even if the result is inevitable, the timing can go awry. The cricketer and publisher Eddie de Vauxhall-Jones, in his Irish Guards days, once found himself in the boxing ring with the Forces champion, Corporal Mike 'the Mongoose' Maclintock, a ferocious Ulsterman about half his height. After a few tentative exchanges, the Mongoose managed to clinch with Eddie and whisper in his ear, 'For God's sake lie down, sir. Lie down, or I'll have to hurt you!' Eddie declined the invitation, and, while he remembers very little of what happened afterwards, is fairly sure that the fight lasted well into the next round.

An altogether rasher challenge was issued by the elegant George Plimpton, actor, belle-lettriste and founder of *The Paris Review*. His chosen adversary was Archie Moore, Light Heavyweight World Champion 1951–9, ranked number 4 in The Ring's '100 greatest punchers of all time'. He gave an account of the event in *Shadow Box*.

As the day of the fight approached, I began to get notes in the mail. I don't know who sent them. Most of them were signed with fighters' names – aphorisms, properly terse, and almost all somewhat violent in tone...

One of them read, "If you get belted and see three fighters through a haze, go after the one in the middle. That's what ruined me – going after the other two guys." – MAX BAER.

Another, on the back of a postcard that had a cat sitting next to a vase of roses on the front, announced succinctly, "Go on in there, he can't hurt us." – LEO P. FLYNN, FIGHT MANAGER.

Another had the curious words Eddie Simms murmured when Art Donovan, the referee, went over to his corner to see how clear-headed he was after being pole-axed by Joe Louis in their Cleveland fight: "Come on, let's take a walk on the roof. I want some fresh air."

Joe Louis' famous remark about Billy Conn turned up one morning: "He can run, but he can't hide." So did James Braddock's description of what it was like to be hit by a Joe Louis jab: "...like someone jammed an electric bulb in your face and busted it."

One of the lengthier messages... read as follows: "Your name is George Plimpton. You have had an appointment with Archie Moore. Your head is now a concert hall where Chinese music will never stop playing."

The last one I received was a short description of a fighter named Joe Dunphy, from Syracuse, a fair middleweight, who became so paralyzed considering his prospects against a top middleweight Australian named Dan Creedon that he stood motionless in his corner at the opening bell, his eyes popping, until finally Creedon, carefully, because he was looking for some kind of trick, went up and knocked him down, much as one might push over a storefront mannequin.

Occasionally, someone of a more practical mind than the mysterious message-sender would call up with a positive word of advice. One of the stranger suggestions was that I avail myself of the services of a spellcaster named Evil Eye Finkel. He possessed what he called the "Slobodka Stare," which he boasted was what had finally finished off Adolf Hitler.

"Think of that," I said.

"Evil Eye's got a manager," I was told. "Name of Mumbles Sober. The pair of them can be hired for fifty dollars to five hundred dollars depending – so it says in the brochure – on the 'wealth of the employer and the difficulty of the job'."

I wondered aloud what the price difference would be between saving my skin in the ring against Archie Moore and what it had cost to preserve the Western democracies from fascism.

"I don't know," I was told. "You'll have to ask Mumbles."

As it was, I picked corner men who were literary rather than evil-eyed, or even pugilistic – composed of the sort of friends one might have as ushers at a wedding (or perhaps, more appropriately, as someone pointed out, as bearers at a funeral) rather than at a boxing showdown in a gymnasium. They were Peter Matthiessen, the novelist and explorer (he appeared on the day of the fight and gave me the tibia of an Arctic hare as a good-luck token – the biggest rabbit's foot I had ever seen); Tom Guinzburg, of the Viking Press; Blair Fuller, the novelist; Bob Silvers, then an editor of Harpers; and, of course, George Brown, the only professional among us, who of course had literary connections because of his friendship with Ernest Hemingway. None of them, except Brown, had anything to do, really. I asked them if they would have lunch with me the day of the fight. They could steady me through the meal and get me to eat something. They could distract me with funny stories.

[...] We had the lunch at the Racquet Club. My friends stared at me with odd smiles. We ordered the meal out of stiff large menus that crackled sharply when opened. I ordered eggs benedict, a steak diane, and a chocolate-ice-cream compote. Someone said that it was not the sort of place, or meal, one would relate to someone going up against the light-heavyweight champion of the world, but I said I was having the meal to quiet my nerves; the elegance of the place, and the food, arriving at the table in silver serving dishes, helped me forget where I was going to be at five that afternoon.

I took out Matthiessen's enormous rabbit foot. "How can I lose with this thing?" I said. We talked about good-luck charms and I said that in the library down the hall I had read that when Tom Sharkey was preparing for a fight against Gus Ruhlin, he was sent a pair of peacocks by Bob Fitzsimmons, the former heavyweight champion. Sharkey was somewhat shaken by the gift, because he said he had heard from an old Irishwoman that an owner of a peacock never had any good luck. But Fitzsimmons was such a good friend that Sharkey didn't want to insult him by sending the birds back. So Sharkey kept them around, walking past their pens rather hurriedly, and indeed when he lost the fight to Ruhlin in the eleventh round, he blamed it on what he called his "Jonah birds".

"*You trying to tell me you feel awkward about that hare's foot?*" *Matthiessen asked.*

I had the sense that he had been reluctant to give it up in the first place. It was a huge foot, and it probably meant a lot to him.

"*Perhaps you could hold it for me,*" *I said.*

"*You better keep it,*" *he said.*

During lunch I kept wondering what Archie Moore was up to. [...]

Later I discovered what he was doing. At the same time I was having lunch with my entourage, he was sitting in a restaurant with Peter Maas, a journalist friend of mine. Over dessert, Archie Moore asked Peter who I was – this fellow he had agreed to go three rounds with later that afternoon. Maas, who knew about the arrangements – I had invited him to Stillman's – could not resist it: he found himself, somewhat to his surprise, describing me to Moore as an "intercollegiate boxing champion."

Once Peter had got that out, he began to warm to his subject. "He's a gawky sort of guy, but don't let that fool you, Arch. He's got a left jab that sticks, he's fast, and he's got a pole-axe left hook that he can really throw. He's a barnburner of a fighter, and the big thing about him is that he wants to be the light heavyweight champion of the world. Very ambitious. And confident. He doesn't see why he should work his way up through all the preliminaries in the tank towns: he reckons he's ready now."

Moore arched his eyebrows at this.

"He's invited all his friends," Maas went on gaily, "a few members of the press, a couple of guys who are going to be at the McNeil Boxing Award dinner tonight" – which was the real reason Moore was in town – and in front of all these people he's going to waltz into the ring and take you. What he's done is to sucker you into the ring."

Maas told me all of this later. He said he had not suspected himself of such satanic capacities; it all came out quite easily.

Moore finally had a comment to offer. "If that guy lays a hand on me I'm going to coldcock him." He cracked his knuckles alarmingly at the table.[...]

At the time, of course, I knew none of this. I dawdled away the afternoon and arrived early at Stillman's. George Brown was with me, carrying his little leather case with the gloves, and some "equipment" he felt he might have to use if things got "difficult" for me up in the ring.

We went up the steps of the building at Eighth Avenue, through the turnstile, and Lou Stillman led us through the back area of his place into an arrangement of dressing cubicles as helter-skelter as a Tangier slum, with George Brown's nose wrinkled up as we were shown back into the gloom and a stall was found. George sat me down in a corner, and, snapping open his kit bag, he got ready to tape my hands. I worried aloud that Archie Moore might not show up, and both George and I laughed at the concern in my voice, as if a condemned prisoner were fretting that the fellow in charge of the dawn proceedings might have overslept. We began to hear people arriving outside, the hum of voices beginning to rise. I had let a number of people know; the word of the strange cocktail-hour exhibition had spread. Blair Fuller arrived. He was the only one of my seconds who seemed willing to identify himself with what was going to go on. The rest said they were going to sit in the back. Fuller was wearing a T-shirt with THE PARIS REVIEW across the front.

Suddenly, Archie Moore himself appeared at the door of my cubicle. He was in his street clothes. He was carrying a kit bag and a pair of boxing gloves; the long white laces hung down loose. There was a crowd of people behind him, peering in over his shoulders – Miles Davis, the trumpet player, one of them; and I thought I recognized Doc Kearns, Moore's legendary manager, with his great ears soaring up the sides of his head and the slight tang of toilet water sweetening the air of the cubicle (he was known for the aroma of his colognes). But all of this was a swift impression, because I was staring up at Moore from my stool. He looked down and said as follows: "Hmm." There were no greetings. He began undressing. He stepped out of his pants and shorts; over his hips he began drawing up a large harnesslike foul-protector. I stared at it in awe. I had not thought to buy one myself; the notion of the champion's throwing a low blow had not occurred to me. Indeed, I was upset to realize he thought I was capable of doing such a thing. "I don't have one of those," I murmured. I don't think he heard me. The man I took to be Doc Kearns was saying, "Arch, let's get on out of here. It's a freak show." Beyond the cubicle we could hear the rising murmur of the crowd.

"No, no, no," I said. "It's all very serious."

Moore looked at me speculatively. "Go out there and do your best," he said. He settled the cup around his hips and flicked its surface with a fingernail; it gave off a dull, tinny sound. He drew on his trunks. He began taping his hands – the shriek of the adhesive drawn in bursts off its spool, the flurry of his fists as he spun the tape around them. During this, he offered us a curious monologue, apparently about a series of victories back in his welterweight days: "I put that guy in the hospital, didn't I? Yeah, banged him around the eyes so it was a question about could he ever see again?" He looked at me again. "You do your best, hear?" I nodded vaguely. He went back to his litany. "Hey, Doc, you remember the guy who couldn't remember his name after we finished with him... just plumb banged that guy's name right out of his skull?" He smoothed the tape over his hands and slid on the boxing gloves. Then he turned and swung a punch at the wall of the cubicle with a force that bounced a wooden medicine cabinet off its peg; it fell to the floor and exploded in a shower of rickety slats.

"These gloves are tight," he said as he walked out. A roll of athletic tape fell out of the ruin of the cabinet

and unravelled across the floor. Beyond the cubicle wall I heard a voice cut through the babble: "Whatever he was, Arch, he was not an elephant."

Could that have been Kearns? An assessment of the opposition? Of course, at the time I had no idea that Peter Maas had built me up into a demonic contender whom they had good reason to check.

[...]

The place was packed; the seats stretching back from the ring (a utility from the days when the great fighters sparred at Stillman's) were full, and behind them people were standing back along the wall. Archie Moore was waiting up in the ring, wearing a white T-shirt and a pair of knit boxing trunks like a 1920s bathing suit. As I climbed into the ring he had his back to me, leaning over the ropes and shouting at someone in the crowd. I saw him club at the ring ropes with a gloved fist, and I could feel the structure of the ring shudder. Ezra Bowen, a Sports Illustrated editor, jumped into the ring to act as referee. He provided some florid instructions, and then waved the two of us together. Moore turned and began shuffling quickly toward me.

[...]

As he moved around the ring he made a curious humming sound in his throat, a sort of peaceful aimless sound one might make pruning a flower bed, except that from time to time the hum would rise quite abruptly, and bang! He would cuff me alongside the head. I would sense the leaden feeling of being hit, the almost acrid whiff of leather off his gloves, and I would blink through the sympathetic response [tears] and try to focus on his face, which looked slightly startled, as if he could scarcely believe he had done such a thing. Then I'd hear the humming again, barely distinguishable now against the singing in my own head.

Halfway through the round Moore slipped – almost to one knee – not because of anything I had done, but his footing had betrayed him somehow. Laughter rose out of the seats, and almost as if in retribution he jabbed and followed with a long lazy left hook that fetched up against my nose and collapsed it slightly. It began to bleed. There was a considerable amount of sympathetic response and though my physical reaction, the jab ("peck, peck, peck"), was thrown in a frenzy and with considerable spirit, the efforts popped up against Moore's guard as ineffectually as I were poking at the side of a barn. The tears came down my cheeks. We revolved around the ring. I could hear the crowd – a vague buzzing – and occasionally I could hear my name being called out: "Hey, George, hit him back; hit him in the knees, George." I was conscious of how inappropriate the name George was to the ring, rather like hearing "Timothy" or "Warren" or "Christopher." Occasionally I was aware of the faces hanging above the seats like rows of balloons, unrecognizable, many of them with faint anticipatory grins on their faces, as if they were waiting for a joke to be told which was going to be pretty good. They were slightly inhuman, I remember thinking, the banks of them staring up, and suddenly into my mind popped a scene from Conan Doyle's The Croxley Master: *his fine description of a fight being watched by Welsh miners, each with his dog sitting behind him; they went everywhere as companions, so that the boxers looked down and everywhere among the human faces were the heads of dogs, yapping from the benches, the muzzles pointing up, the tongues lolling.*

We went into a clinch; I was surprised when I was pushed away and saw the sheen of blood on Moore's T-shirt. Moore looked slightly alarmed. The flow of tears was doubtless disarming. He moved forward and enfolded me in another clinch. He whispered in my ear, "Hey, breathe, man, breathe." The bell sounded and I turned from him and headed for my corner, feeling very much like sitting down.

[...]

For the next two rounds Moore let up considerably, being assured – if indeed it had ever worried him – of the quality of his opposition. In the last round he let me whale away at him from time to time, and then he would pull me into a clinch and whack at me with great harmless popping shots to the backs of my shoulder blades which sounded like the crack of artillery. Once I heard him ask Ezra Bowen if he was behind on points.

But George Brown and Blair Fuller did not like what was going on at all... I think mostly because of the unpredictable nature of my opponent: his moods seemed to change as the fight went on; he was evidently not quite sure how to comport himself – clowning for a few seconds, and then the humming would rise, and they would grimace as a few punches were thrown with more authority; they could see my mouth drop ajar. In the third round Brown began to feel that Moore had run through as much of a repertoire as he could devise, and that the fighter, wondering how he could finish things off aesthetically, was getting testy about it. I was told Tom Guinzburg, one of my seconds, came up to the corner and threw a towel into the ring... but whether he was doing it because he was worried or because he knew it would raise a laugh – which indeed it did – I never discovered. But, long after the event, I found out that Brown had reached down and advanced the hand of the time clock. The bell clanged sharply with a good minute to go. Ezra called us together to raise both our arms, and, funning it up, he called the affair a draw. I can remember the relief of its being done, vaguely worried that it had not been more conclusive, or artistic; I was quite grateful for the bloody nose.

8

THE NEW OLYMPIAN

All sports can be practised decadently. One thinks of Alfred Jarry's bicycling, of Donald Crowhurst going mad on his phantom round-the-world voyage, of Big Bill Tilden, the tennis star, imprisoned for having sex with a 14-year-old in a moving vehicle on Sunset Boulevard... There are shadow armies of magnificently perverted footballers, racing drivers, marksmen, golfers, alpinistes, baseballers, tennis-players, dart-flingers and billiardeurs, not to mention the devotees of more exotic sports such as elephant polo, bandy and *varzesh-e bastani* – regal souls for whom the contest is a chariot driven by their demons in which they are merely the wild-eyed passengers.

Sport, once a savage, unruly activity, has been seized, disinfected, and shackled by bourgeois rectitude. Rules and numbers proliferate. Science is king. The poetry of sport has been trampled underfoot by the mindless herd.

It should not be thus. Just as gardens are a living connection with the agricultural past and the wild landscapes where we used to hunt and gather and fornicate, so the sports field must connect us with ancient rituals of blood sacrifice, kingship, war, sexual potency, communion with the gods of earth, air, water and fire.

Our old friend Freddie Nietzsche saw life as a *lucha libre* between Apollo and Dionysos, the one rational and controlled, the other wild and impulsive. History is a cycle, in which the forces of restriction and freedom, stupidity and intelligence, alternate endlessly and pointlessly.

We propose a new Dionysiac Olympics, liberated from the dull conformism of the official model. Is the world not weary of machine-like athletes performing repetitive tasks against the clock? Of commercially sponsored muscle? Do our hordes of workers and peasants not yearn for something more chaotic, more explosive, more baroque? In a word, more Decadent?

A number of alternatives to the Olympic Games already exist. Robert Dover's Cotswold Olimpicks have been celebrated in Gloucestershire each year at Pentecost since 1612, with English country sports such as gurning, shin-kicking, tug of war and cock-strangling. In Greece a spectre of the antique games is revived four-yearly in the stadium of Nemea, near Corinth, where pine branches blaze on the altar, heralds announce the races in ancient tongues, amateurs run barefoot, and the winners are crowned with wreaths of wild celery. Medlar was scheduled to run in these very games in the summer of 2012: he turned up in plaid golfing trousers, purple brogues and a cream serge cricket shirt, only to be disqualified when he refused to remove his shoes.

Closer to the Decadent spirit is The Chap Olympiad, 'a celebration of eccentricity and athletic ineptitude' under the impeccable supervision of Gustav Temple, boulevardier and dandy. This is a bold rethinking of an ancient concept, bringing the Chappist ideal of British gentlemanly attire, coiffure and manners into the sporting arena. It is infinitely more faithful to Baron de Coubertin's vision of amateurism than anything done in his name by international committees. This is the programme for 2011:

1.30 pm Opening Ceremony
The lighting of the Olympic Pipe.

2.00 pm Martini Knockout Relay
The object is to mix the perfect dry martini, using gin, vermouth, ice, cocktail shaker and olive or lemon peel. Each stage of the mixing is carried out by one of the four members of each of the six teams. The final drink is tasted and judged by a connoisseur.

2.30 pm Cucumber Sandwich Discus
Individuals must hurl a cucumber sandwich on a china plate. The object is for the sandwich to land with the minimum distance from the plate. The shortest distance betwixt plate and sandwich wins. The sandwich must remain intact and without too much earth or other matter inside it. The crusts are naturally removed before the game commences so as not to offend the participants.

3.00 pm Umbrella Jousting
A rope is tethered between two hat stands. Two chaps on bicycles must knock each other off using brollies. They carry shields made of reinforced copies of broadsheet newspapers. The winner is the first chap to knock the other chap off his velocipede.

3.30 pm Tug of Hair
Michael "Atters" Attree sits in a leather armchair with a 20-foot moustache. Teams of ten or more tug at either end, until one team emerges victorious by yanking the other team to the ground, or de-whiskerading Atters.

THE DECADENT SPORTSMAN

4.00 pm Break For Tiffin

5.00 pm Hop, Skip and G&T
Each contestant must hop, skip and jump carrying a full tumbler of gin and tonic. The remains of the drink are measured and the one with the most drink in the glass wins.

5.30 pm The Pipeathlon
This event is done in pairs of athletes at a time (rather than using all six lanes). The track is roughly divided into 3 sections of 4 yards each. Each contestant must complete the first 4 yards with a lit pipe, the second on a bicycle and the third without touching the ground, which can be achieved any way they like (usually carried by their chums). Up to six pairs of contestants can take part.

6.00 pm Three-Trousered Limbo
Pairs of contestants are strapped into huge pairs of double trousers. The limbo pole is placed half way along the track. They must shimmy under it, then the pole is lowered slightly and the next pair must shimmy even lower. Points are awarded purely for panache.

6.30 pm Bounders
The ladies all line up at the finishing line. One by one, each bounder approaches them and whispers something to one of the ladies. She responds, usually with a slap. The most violent response gives the cad the most points. This event benefits from a horse-racing commentary-style approach.

7.00 pm The Grand Steeplechase
Six chaps wear animal masks. Six ladies mount them, carrying riding crops. There are a series of picket fences along the track which they must jump (with rather poor visibility). The winner is first past the post. The race will be run several times, to give everyone a chance at it.

Short break announced by MC while the judges make their decisions (inspecting trouser creases/measuring gaps between tie and shirt collar etc).

8.00 pm Prize giving ceremony
The gold, silver and bronze cravats are awarded to the three contestants who have shown the most verve, panache and skullduggery throughout the day.

The Chap Olympics (and its latest appendage, the Paralyticolympics) may be a recent invention, but it has the weight of history behind it. The English gentleman introduced sports to a world that was desperately hungry for them. Entire civilisations had languished in spiritual poverty for millennia for want of such things as a decent round of golf, the cry of 'How's that?' among the baobabs, or the scrimmaging of soldiers and administrators in colonial mud. Natives were taught to play cricket and tennis, fives and rugby, to appreciate the meaning of teamwork, sportsmanship, fair play and triangular fish paste sandwiches, and to regard sport as a training for war, business, marriage, child-rearing and politics. The natives' efforts were politely encouraged, until they became better than their masters, at which point full political independence was granted. Sporting associations sprang up like dandelions in every corner of the Empire. One need only think of the Muthaiga, the Hong Kong Ping Pong Club, the Cairo Beagle Pack, the Ski Club of Nyasaland... all with their own club-houses, cufflinks, ties, whist drives and adulteries. Stirring examples to those less fortunate than ourselves.

The greatest of imperial sports is, in our view, cricket: a game that requires the transformation of the landscape, not merely the culture, of different climate zones, so that they accurately reproduce the verdant meadows of the British Isles – no small achievement in Afghanistan or West Africa. Unique among sports, cricket has an almost Buddhistic calm about its proceedings, which, with its minimal physical demands and leisurely agricultural timescale, permits even the most unathletic to take part in its mysterious rites.

Nothing illustrates this more poignantly than a match that took place at the Montpelier Gardens, Walworth, in 1796, 'to be played by eleven Greenwich pensioners with one leg against eleven with one arm', for a prize of a thousand guineas. It attracted an enormous crowd. *About nine o'clock,* reports Pierce Egan:

> *the men arrived in three Greenwich stages; about ten the wickets were pitched, and the match commenced. Those with but one leg had the first innings, and got ninety-three runs. About three o'clock, while those with but one arm were having their innings, a scene of riot and confusion took place, owing to the pressure of the populace to gain admittance: the gates were forced open, parts of the fencing broke down, and a great number of persons having got upon the top of a stable, the roof*

broke in, and many were taken out much bruised. About six o'clock the game was renewed, and those with one arm got but forty-two runs during their innings. The one legs commenced their second innings, and six were bowled out after they got sixty runs, so that they left off one hundred and eleven more than those with one arm.

The match was played again on the Wednesday following, and the men with one leg beat the one arms by one hundred and three runs. After the match was finished, the eleven one-legged men ran one hundred yards for twenty guineas. The three first divided the money.

The British however cannot claim to have invented all the world's great sports. The Italians bequeathed us pigeon racing. This working-class pursuit, connected by invisible threads to occult forces of nature, relies on the pigeon's uncanny ability to find its way home over huge distances without the benefit of a map. The birds are gathered, released simultaneously, and then fly home as fast as they can. Although it sounds simple, straightforward and honest, it's a magnificently dirty sport, as recalled by the pilot and wildlife photographer Egidio Gavazzi in his book *Desiderio di volo:*

At school I had a friend who kept racing pigeons. His uncle, the baker, had owned Anello d'Oro, the Italian champion... My friend lived in a little house at the edge of the village. Jutting from its roof was the pigeon loft, a small square construction. Here the racers lived, and my friend and I spent interminable hours. The eggs arrived by air mail from Belgium, carefully selected and authenticated by the breeder's stamp. My friend showed me the art of slipping thoroughbred eggs into the nests of farmyard pigeons, which would hatch them, believing them to be their own. The legitimate eggs, if they were fresh, we drank...

A keen apprentice to his uncle, my friend used the meanest of tricks to improve his team's performance. Before sending off his best birds to a race, he would show them their partners in company with the most unpopular bachelors and spinsters of the colony. The legitimate spouses would go flat out for home, and, once back, hurl themselves at their rivals, real or presumed, despite their exhaustion. We were there waiting, with the twofold aim of recording their race times and removing our champions from an inevitable mauling by well-rested foes. Bitter currents of hatred divided that community as a result of our actions.

We can't help thinking that a similar strategy might be used to add a modicum of interest to the men's and women's marathon.

A New Olympic Programme

Having thus established the need for root and branch reform, we propose an entirely new Olympic enterprise, based on our lifelong commitment to the Caligulisation of human existence. As the world's leading thinkers in this field, it falls to us to dictate the new order of events in all their details. But effective reform must begin at the top. We will replace the herds of faceless functionaries who have laid the dead hand of bureaucracy on world sport with a slimmed-down *nomenklatura* of two. From the new IOC headquarters in Havana we have already begun to sketch out our vision of the Decadent Games:

> Day 1: Opening Ceremony in the Spartan Style, with a parade of athletes, nude, oiled and lightly powdered with golden dust.
> Day 2: Roman Games, with Chariot Racing, Hunting and Gladiator Combat
> Day 3: Orgies & Feasts
> Day 4: Hangover Cricket and Horse Racing
> Day 5: Gluttony and Cocktail Mixing
> Day 666: Bestial Transgression Day (Crowley Memorial Games)
> Day 7: Aerial Olympics & Urban Exploration
> Day 8: The Chap Olympiad
> Day 9: Amateur Dentistry and Russian Roulette
> Day 10: Sexual Olympics and Endurance Voyeurism
> Day 11: Duelling
> Day 12: Bohemian Triathlon: Extravagance, Unreliability, Disorderliness
> Day 13: S & M Swimming
> Day 14: Hairdressing and Wild Boar Hunting
> Day 15: Posing, Dandyism & Couture
> Day 16: Mind Games and Closing Ceremony

The Rules of the New Olympics

These are simplicity itself.
1) The nation offering the largest bribe gets the games.
2) Style is everything.

Questions of doping and other forms of cheating, which have bedevilled sport from the start, will now be irrelevant. Thanks to Rule 2, victory (in the sense of coming first in races) is pointless, so dishonest means to achieve it are also pointless; such things will simply wither away. Cheating *stylishly*, however, must be rewarded.

The mistake that sports administrators are making at present is in trying to stamp out dishonesty. We are of the opinion that it should be celebrated in all its forms. These often bring much-needed imaginative thinking and innovation to sport. Those who get caught cheating should of course be punished for their incompetence. They would be presented with the Boris Onischenko Award for Incompetent Dishonesty, named in honour of the Russian pentathlete who in the 1976 Olympics rigged his epée so that it registered a hit even when he was standing en garde. He was duly expelled from the games and his team lost their gold medal. We are of the opinion that such punishment is hardly sufficient. A more imaginative way of dealing with Boris would have been to bury him up to his neck in the javelin field somewhere between the Olympic and the World record distance and let him take his chances. This is how the Mogul emperors would have dealt with such transgression.

Another crude instance of cheating was provided by figure skater, Tonya Harding, and her role in the 1994 knee-capping of her rival, Nancy Kerrigan. She denied involvement but was convicted of perverting the course of justice. Perverting the course of anything is to be applauded but Harding's antics were crass and distinctly unstylish. Little wonder that she ended up involved in a series of minor court cases, a celebrity sex tape scandal and a hugely unsuccessful career as a boxer.

A more appropriate example of New Olympian cheating

is that of East German athlete, Horst Maier, who knowing that he stood no chance against the Uruguayan wrestler, Alejandro Macerata, in the final of the 1968 World Greco-Roman Wrestling championships, slipped a derivative of anabolic steroid into his opponent's drinking water before the contest. Macerata duly won their encounter, tested positive for a substance he did not know he had taken, and was stripped of his title, which was immediately handed to Maier. Macerata died in disgrace and poverty back in Montevideo while Maier became President of the GDR Wrestling Federation, was awarded the Walter Honecker Medal and died peacefully in his bed at an advanced age. His subterfuge only came to light many years later when his wife defected to the West and went to the press to recount the story of her husband's actions.

Dress Code

The athletes' parade will introduce a new Olympic couture. As a farewell to the vulgarity of lycra and a stimulus to the revival of bespoke athletic tailoring, competitors will be encouraged to think of themselves as moving works of art. (The New Olympic committee might co-opt Gilbert and George and Grayson Perry to advise on performance sportswear design). For sculling we look to Oscar Wilde who, while staying at Goring-on-Thames in August 1893, wore a pale blue shirt with a pale pink silk tie: 'colours,' notes Richard Ellman, 'which the next day he would reverse. He used a white lilac perfume.'

For waterskiing, javelin and pigeon-racing we suggest the speckmantel, a coat of linen hung with slices of raw ham, as worn by Durian Gray during the summer season at Bregenz in 2008 (see the title page of this chapter). This exquisite garment is as fragrant as it is elegant, a triumph of synaesthesia, sexual magnetism and impracticality. However, it should not be worn in the vicinity of hungry dogs, lest an Acteon-style incident be precipitated.

A three-piece suit in tweed or linen, silk cravat, crocodile shoes and fez are highly suitable for track and field events, both male and female. The fez has fine aerodynamic qualities which will improve any athletic performance. Naval uniforms look good on cyclists. A bullfighter's *traje de luces* will not go amiss in swimming. Wrestling in smoking-jackets is always a pleasure to watch. To the practised eye, the history of tailoring is a goldmine of possibilities.

Now for a few more details of the events:

Opening Ceremony
The preferred director of proceedings is the Russian underground film-maker, scrap-metal dealer and wedding photographer Zoltan Zukofsky. No other stage or screen director can match Zukofsky's mastery of chaos spectacle, cacophony, shock tactics and bad taste on the grand scale: he describes his aesthetic vision as 'porno-mafia-schizo-cosmic breakdown art', and promises to create 'an opening ceremony that will make the Day of Judgement look like a tea party for old maids'.

Bestial Transgression
Show-jumping and dressage are, as things stand, the only Olympic sports requiring the participation of animals. The Decadent Olympics will have many more. Apart from Pigeon Racing, we have plans for a 4 x 400-metre Whale Relay, Tortoise Dressage (Jewelled and Plain), Baboon Archery and Python Wrestling. In the spirit of opennness there will be an

all-comers event, with no restrictions on eligibility.

The concept of Bestial Transgression is simple. A formal parade of animals, somewhat like Cruft's Dog Show, in which elegance of presentation, control, obedience, grace of movement, etc. are strictly marked by a punctilious team of judges. To score highly, however, and hope to win a medal, the animal must transgress in some way – the more grotesque the better. A turd laid in front of the judges is a good beginning. Several turds is better. A stream of urine will do almost as well, more so if it is against an official's leg. World class is achieved by exceptional transgressions only, such as the stallion Petroleum King, who, half way through a round of dressage in Kentucky, spotted an attractive mare on heat and decided that he would rather climb onto her and claim his seigneurial rights than continue mincing sideways across a meadow. He resisted all attempts to drag him off, and completed a very public orgasm while his rider, a young lady-in-waiting to the Queen of Denmark, managed miraculously to stay in the saddle. Not every horse is a Petroleum King, of course, but his great example stands for all to follow.

Urban Exploration
Here is a sport bursting with decadent credentials. Urban explorers work at night, penetrating secret and forbidden areas of the city. They are vertical transgressors, climbing locked buildings, descending into subterranean passages and caverns, forgotten railway stations, quarries, sewers, tunnels, bunkers. La Mexicaine de Perforation ran an underground cinema and bar under the Palais de Chaillot in Paris. They wandered through miles of galleries, tunnels and ancient quarries beneath the city, to 'reclaim and transform disused urban spaces for the creation of zones of expression for free and independent

art.' Meanwhile The London Consolidation Crew have been trespassing gaily over the roofs of the British Museum and St Paul's Cathedral, the Shard, Battersea Power Station, and through London's sewers and derelict underground railway stops. 'The motivation is about seeing things that are hidden from view,' says their ideologue Bradley Garrett, aligning the sport firmly with another, more ancient and venerable Decadent sport: voyeurism.

In a marriage of Old and New Olympics, we will stage a sewer triathlon, threading the underground tunnels and sluiceways of the city in an event that combines swimming, horse-racing and running in magnificently putrid surroundings. Only when sport quits the sun-filled stadia or flood-lit arenas and begins to explore the ludic possibilities of dark, subterranean spaces will it be able to begin to consider itself truly Decadent.

And the alternative to the New Olympics? The alternative is surely an increasingly grotesque form of what is served up daily by corporations, TV companies and functionaries as a soporific to the common man, to make him forget the ugliness of his existence. Perec has already seen the future of sportsmen:

> *The life of an Athlete of W is nothing but one endless, furious striving, a pointless, debilitating pursuit of that unreal moment when triumph brings rest. How many hundreds, how many thousands of hours of crushing effort for one second of serenity, one second of calm? How many weeks, how many months of exhaustion for one hour of relaxation?*

And with terrifying perspicacity he shows us the logical outcome of this relentless pursuit of sporting excellence – the W Olympic Games itself:

Bands decked out in sparkling uniforms play Beethoven's Ninth. Thousands of doves and coloured balloons are released into the air. Behind enormous, fluttering standards displaying the interlocking circles, the Gods of the Stadium process on to the track in impeccable columns, their arms extended towards the official boxes where the great Dignitaries of W acknowledge them.

If you just look at the Athletes, if you just look: in their striped kit they look like caricatures of turn-of-the-century sportsmen as, with their elbows in, they lunge into a grotesque sprint; if you just look at the shot-putters, who have cannonballs for shot, or at the jumpers with their ankles tied together, or at the long jumpers landing heavily in a sandpit filled with manure; if you just look at the wrestlers, tarred and feathered, if you just look at the long-distance runners running three-legged or on all fours, if you just look at the knackered, shivering survivors of the marathon, hobbling between two serried ranks of Line Judges armed with sticks and cudgels, if you just look and see these Athletes of skin and bone, ashen-faced, their backs permanently bent, their skulls bald and shiny, their eyes full of panic, and their suppurating sores, if you see all those permanent marks of relentless humiliation, of boundless terror, all of it evidence, administered every hour, every day, every moment, of conscious, organised, structured oppression; if you just look and see the workings of this huge machine, each cog of which contributes with implacable efficiency to the systematic annihilation of men, then it should come as no great surprise that the performances put in are totally mediocre: the 100 metres is run in 23.4 seconds, the 200 metres in 51 seconds; the best high jumper has never exceeded 1.30 metres.

9

MIND GAMES

By now even the most *zombifié* of readers will have come to the conclusion that is not the sport itself that counts in the Decadent Olympics so much as the *mind of the sportsman*. When Swinburne went swimming in rough seas, he was taking his mind as much as his body for a mauling. The violence implied in the word 'breakers' unfurled in his brain with a deeply satisfying aggression, and continued to do so long after he had finished dabbing iodine on his cuts.

The mind is the invisible contestant at each sporting encounter. Its interventions, like the Roman emperors' thumb signals, are decisive. A mass of books and articles on 'the inner game' (of tennis, golf, business, skiing, sex, etc) testifies to this. 'The inner game,' says one of its proponents, 'takes place within the mind of the player and is played against such obstacles as fear, self-doubt, lapses in focus, and limiting concepts or assumptions.' (How often have we cheered ourselves on with such thoughts, finding courage up the most hopeless of creeks, playing that inner game even when the bailiffs are at the door or the police are unbelting their handcuffs...)

Although the goal is 'focus', the trick of achieving it is often to be found in distraction and contrariness. The coiner of the phrase 'the inner game' was Timothy Gallwey. Combining his experience as captain of the Harvard tennis team with a system of meditation learned in India, he found ways to fool the brain into improved performance in spite of itself. Instead of instructing a player to keep his eye on the ball, he taught them to say 'bounce' every time the ball bounced and 'hit' every time they struck it. While distracted by this nursery-school naming game, the mind, that most fickle of pupils, focussed effortlessly on the trajectory of the ball.

An old tennis-player's ruse, much used by Durian Gray in his days as a hustler at the Buenos Aires Lawn Tennis Club, is to compliment your opponent on a fine shot. This puts him under pressure to do it again, vastly lessening the probability that he will. When his next shot hits the net, more stress is piled on as he wonders why he has failed to measure up to his own high standards. He begins to think too much. Thus he is quickly reduced to a neurotic wreck.

The subtlety of the poisoned compliment becomes evident when we compare it to the counterproductive power of the insult, which only serves to increase the opponent's aggression. Richard Hilary, in *The Last Enemy*, recalls a rowing match in Germany when the Oxford crew, having failed to train on anything other than beer, cigarettes and shortage of sleep, earned the contempt of the locals for their slovenly and unsportsmanlike appearance. As the boat passed under a bridge, a spectator spat on them. This, says Hilary, was a mistake. Fired up with anger, they flung away their nonchalance and beat the German boat decisively.

In cricket, that most gentlemanly of sports, there is a special term for a verbal technique designed to get inside the mind of your opponent, making them feel self-conscious or lose concentration, reducing their self-confidence to zero. It is called 'sledging'. An early example comes from a match between the Free Foresters and Cambridge University at Fenners in 1906 when the Hon. Edward de Vere, keeping wicket, made the following remark to the batsman: "I understand your mother serves her guests *Indian* tea." The batsman, Johnny Langdon-Phipps, replied that at least his mother didn't have to do her own shopping. The gloves came off and the two men had to be separated by the umpires.

Charting the history of sledging one can see with depressing clarity how much the quality of exchanges has deteriorated over time. This process of deterioration accelerated dramatically when the technique became widely adopted by Australian cricketers. In the 1930s when England captain Douglas Jardine complained to the Australian captain Bill Woodfull that a member of his side had called him a bastard, Woodfull turned to his men and asked, "Which one of you bastards called this bastard a bastard?"

Nowadays any semblance of decorum has disappeared. Thus Rodney Marsh to Ian Botham in an Ashes match: "So how's your wife and my kids?", to which Botham replied: "The wife's fine. The kids are retarded."

In cricket's Golden Age of course, before it was corrupted by professionalism, it was more likely that the captain would turn to one of his own teammates and ask: 'How's your wife and my children?' out of genuine concern. And the reply would probably have been: 'All well, thank you, your Lordship. The missus is expecting you Friday."

As the Marsh/Botham repartee shows, the great danger of sledging is that it can easily backfire on the sledger. Australian fast bowler Glen McGrath tried to upset West Indian Ramnaresh Sarwan by asking him what Brian Lara's dick tasted like. Sarwan said he didn't know but that McGrath's wife might. McGrath himself appears to have lost his own cool at this point because he retorted: 'If you ever fucking mention my wife again, I'll fucking rip your fucking throat out.' Antipodean drollery at its finest!

There is one sport where such trading of insults is not an adjunct to competition, but the very essence. It is referred to as the Dozens. The contestants face one another in front of a group of bystanders and exchange insults, questioning each other's intelligence, looks, abilities, personal hygiene, family history ('Your mother eats shit!' 'Your mother eats shit with mustard!' etc). The aim is twofold: to make your opponent lose his *sangfroid*, and to keep your own. The mind is challenged both for inventiveness and self-control – a curious partnership of Dionysian and Apollonian energies. A sense of humour comes in handy. This links the Dozens with *sanankuya*, or cousinage, an important concept in West African societies, as well as many sports clubs around the world, for whom the best relationships are characterised by jokes at each other's expense.

There are several games which exercise intellectual skills – contests of memory, mental arithmetic, chess, Go, etc – but these are of scant interest to the Decadent, who is usually too intoxicated to compete. True mind games involve a form of psychological warfare between opponents, in which bluff, double bluff, triple bluff and all the subsequent illusions and counter-illusions are multiplied in the infinite hall of mirrors of the mind. The game, the real games, consists in knowing which of the million illusions works best for you.

It seems fitting to close this account with the words of the ocean-going sailor Donald Crowhurst. His last entry in the logbook of *Teignmouth Electron,* the trimaran in which he had set off to win the first solo non-stop round the world race, is a poem addressed to God. Having borrowed heavily to finance his voyage, Crowhurst needed to win first prize to avoid financial ruin. He set out late, in an unfinished boat, and, with little hope of achieving his goal, conceived a plan to fake the longest and most hazardous section of the course: 13,000 miles sailing east from the south Atlantic, around the Cape of Good Hope, past Australia and New Zealand, to Cape Horn. Between January and June 1969, Crowhurst moochedalong the coasts of Brazil and Uruguay, plotting a record-breaking streak across the Southern Ocean with fictional daily positions. His boat was damaged and leaking badly. He put into a tiny Brazilian port, Rio Salado, on his way south, and sat out the days, sending radio messages that charted spectacular progress, until he could plausibly rejoin the race. As the crucial moment approached, he realised that a lifetime of lying would be required to sustain his fictional achievement. His mind began to turn. In the last week of June, while heading for home, he gave up trying to sail his boat. Instead he filled his logbook with a raving torrent of apocalyptic thought, explaining to himself that by the power of 'creative abstraction' anything is possible: a great Decadent insight.

On July 1, having forgotten to wind his clocks for a week, with no idea where he was, either in space or time, but guessing it must be about ten in the morning, he made his final entries:

EXACT POS   July 1 10 03

10 23 40   Cannot see any 'purpose' in game.

10 29 00   No game man can devise
             is harmless. The truth is that there
             can only be one chess master...
             there can only be one perfect beauty
             that is the great beauty of truth.
             No man may do more than all

THE DECADENT SPORTSMAN

that he is capable of doing. The perfect
way is the way of reconciliation
Once there is a possibility of reconciliation
there may not be a need for making
errors. Now is revealed the true
nature and purpose and power
of the game my offence I am
I am what I am and I
see the nature of my offence

I will only resign this game
if you will agree that
the next occasion that this
game is played it will be played
according to the
rules that are devised by
my great god who has
revealed at last to his son
not only the exact nature
of the reason for games but
has also revealed the truth of
the way of the ending of the
next game that
     It is finished –
     It is finished
IT IS THE MERCY

11 15 00 It is the end of my
    my game the truth
    has been revealed and it will
    be done as my family require me
    to do it

THE DECADENT SPORTSMAN

11 17 00   It is the time for your
            move to begin.

            I have not need to prolong
            the game

            It has been a good game that
            must be ended at the

            I will play this game when
            I choose I will resign the
            game

11 20 40   There is
            no reason for harmful

Having reached the end of the page he laid down his pen. He unscrewed a chronometer from the bulkhead, and, clutching it to him, jumped into the sea.

This whole strange episode would make a perfect closing event to the New Olympics, with points awarded by the judges for poetic invention, choice of object, tool handling, and style in the final jump. The *salto mortale,* or leap of death, closes the Games, as it closes the metaphor of life.

ACKNOWLEDGEMENTS

We salute the noble souls who have helped us in the writing of this book: most particularly Piers Pottinger, William Martin, Sir Anthony Weldon, Tom Guest and Tony Ortega of *The Village Voice*.

We thank those authors, publishers and literary agents who have kindly granted us permission to quote from their works: Egidio Gavazzi *(Desiderio di Volo)*, Nigel Spivey *(The Ancient Olympics)*, Gustav Temple *(The Chap Olympiad)*, Random House Publishers for *W* by Georges Perec and *Waterlog* by Roger Deakin, and David Godwin Associates for *Haunts of the Black Masseur* by Charles Sprawson.

We greet again all those – agents, publishers, authors – whom we have asked for permission to quote, but who have not found it possible to reply. Silence is tricky to interpret, but we take it as a sign of assent, and thank them in their absence. Those whom we have failed utterly to reach, we invite to contact our publisher, George ('the Terminator') Barrington, or, if you are passing through Havana, to drop in at El Periquito for a glass of rum. Señora Carmela, our patron and bankruptcy administrator, will be pleased to give you a memorable evening.

THE AUTHORS

Medlar Lucan and Durian Gray are the authors and protagonists of a cumulative history of bad behaviour, beginning with their days as proprietors of the Decadent Restaurant in Edinburgh, where they recreated for a select clientele the most extravagant, bizarre and transgressive dishes known to mankind. (These were recorded in *The Decadent Cookbook*). After the restaurant was closed on grounds of moral hygiene by the city council, they set off on a Grand Tour of self-imposed exile, the events of which are recounted in *The Decadent Traveller*. They fetched up on the coast of Ireland as guests of Mrs Conchita Gordon where they designed, but failed to build, one of the world's great decadent gardens. This was the subject of *The Decadent Gardener*. Since 2000 they have lived at El Periquito, a cabaret/brothel above a boxing gymnasium in Havana, in whose perfumed halls they have founded and written the annals of *The Hell Fire Touring Club*. Most recently, after exhaustive research in bathing establishments, race tracks, libraries and locker-rooms, they have produced a fourth volume in their magnum opus, *The Decadent Sportsman*.

Alex Martin and Jerome Fletcher have now edited four books by Lucan and Gray for Dedalus, bringing order to a mass of chaotic paperwork and sparing future textual scholars from psychic meltdown. Conforming precisely to Dr Johnson's definition of the lexicographer, they are harmless drudges, content to live in modest obscurity, one in London, the other in Devon, while the authors run wild around the more savage shores of experience.

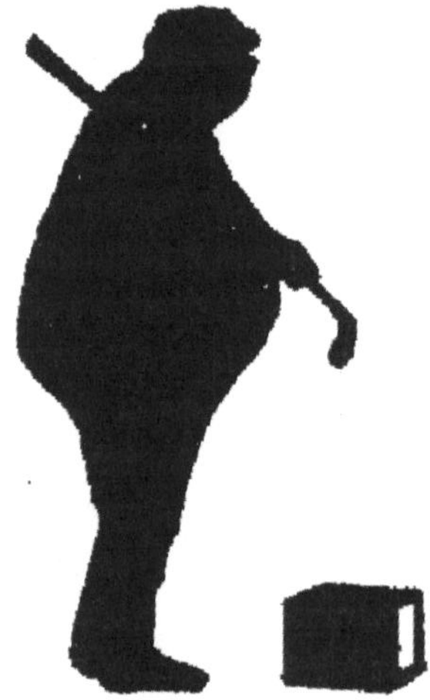